The Whispering House

by

Marci Baun

I0540913

Freya's Bower.com ©2016
Culver City, CA

Chapter One

The enticing aroma of fresh coffee filled the small kitchen. Eleanor breathed deeply and poured herself a cup before crossing to the white Formica table set up beyond the end of the kitchen counter and past the backdoor. It contrasted nicely with the sunshine yellow walls. A cliché, she knew, and not exactly the current decorating trend, but the color always lightened her frequent gloomy moods. This morning was no different. Contentment stole over her, and she pushed back the ever-present sadness that lingered like a dark miasma since her mother's death.

Idly, she doodled on the newspaper in front of her, only half interested in the Sudoku puzzle she'd started to pass time while the coffee finished brewing. With a shake of her head, she set down her pencil and gave up trying to figure out how to fix it so the last square worked with the rest. Instead, she looked through her window at the thick, swirling mist.

The mist shifted as if disturbed by something. Standing, she stepped closer to the window, her mug cradled in her hands. *Was that a figure standing on a path just across the creek? Wait a minute... What path?* She'd taken numerous walks over the past week and had never seen a path there before nor another person since her arrival. Unease slithered along her skin, but she shook it off. She'd been enjoying her solitude, not surveying the countryside.

For several minutes, she stared at the figure, trying to discern whether it was male or female. It was so still; perhaps it didn't really exist or was just a bush she hadn't noticed until now. If only she hadn't left her glasses on the nightstand, she might be able to see a little better.

A patch of fog drifted between her and the figure. The fog writhed and twirled then floated away. The figure was gone, but the path remained. Something didn't seem right. She closed her hand over the doorknob, the desire to find out what was out there nearly overwhelming her.

She glanced at the clock over the sink. It was only three

o'clock, but, after a week of living out here, she knew the fog could roll in early and fast. Before moving to Fresno, she'd heard about the San Joaquin Valley fog, but hadn't believed the tales. Now she did. It'd be better to wait until the morning. The night before, the fog had hugged her small house so tightly that it reflected back the illumination from her porch light, blinding her, reminiscent of the white outs from her childhood vacations up in Lake Tahoe during snowstorms.

With one last look out of the window, she banished any more thoughts of the figure and returned to the table, sitting down and sighing with pleasure. How lovely to relax! Months of dealing with lawyers, tying up the loose ends, selling her family home... Her mind stalled on the last thought. Her aunt's voice filled her head, "Eleanor, you really shouldn't be making such a big decision after only eight months. Everyone knows it's best to wait a year before..."

"I know, Aunt Shirley, but you heard the lawyers. How do you propose I pay the estate taxes? I do well as a financial advisor, but not *that* well. There really isn't any choice. With this sale, I can invest what's left over and retire."

"Are you sure you want to retire and move to..." Distaste flitted across her aunt's face. "Fresno?"

"Yes. It's affordable, quiet and nothing like San Jose." She stopped short of adding "beautiful." Her aunt Shirley would never admit to anything about Fresno being beautiful.

But to Eleanor, even the San Joaquin Valley Tule fog that had blanketed the area since her arrival was beautiful. She hadn't known what to expect with the fog, but she knew she hadn't planned on falling in love with the silvery mist, too. Good thing she had since it was always there. She certainly couldn't tell her aunt that.

Tears welled up in her eyes as she returned to the present. Next to losing both of her parents within two years of each other, having to sell her family home was one of the most difficult things she'd done in her life. The hardest was cleaning out the house, giving away what she couldn't take with her, storing the rest, and reliving all the memories of her parents before she was ready. She hadn't had any time to grieve.

"You are not alone. You are never alone," a man's voice

whispered.

She spun around in her seat, her heart skittering. Who said that? She scanned the interior of her kitchen. Nothing. She walked into the living room. It was empty, too. She moved into the bedroom and shivered. Cold air swirled around her. Strange. There'd never been a draft before. Something wavered in her peripheral vision. She jerked her head toward the movement; her breath caught in her throat. The window was wide open, and the curtains fluttered in the encroaching fog.

Eleanor couldn't move; her feet refused to obey her brain's command and cross to the window. Her unease crashed over her like an avalanche down a steep ravine. Someone had been in her house. Was it the figure from the fog? She shook her head. She didn't want to believe someone watched her.

"Get a grip, Eleanor."

Besides, who would want to break into her house? But what other explanation was there? With a deep breath to gather her courage, she strode to the window and searched the flowerbed beneath it for something—anything—to indicate someone had been there. Nothing was disturbed, not even a footprint in the dirt or the tall grass that passed for her lawn. Nor was there anyone to be seen anywhere. She yanked the window shut, securing the lock. A dark pall of fear settled heavily upon her, and she struggled to breath.

Pulling the curtains shut, she stepped away from the window and rubbed her arms. Shivers rippled through her. Her legs collapsed, she dropped to the floor, and her back collided with the side of the bed.

Wave upon wave of grief consumed her. She gasped for air as the reality of her situation descended upon her. Great rasping sobs shook her body. She shuddered and cried, memories of her parents that she'd locked away rushed over her. And she knew that if anything happened to her out here, no one would know. No one would care. No matter what that whisper claimed, she was truly alone.

Tears trickled down her cheeks intermittently, and she reached for a tissue on her nightstand to blow her nose. The phone beckoned to her.

Before she could change her mind, she snatched it up and

punched in her best friend's number. She tried to wipe away the last traces of tears as the phone rang. The answering machine picked up. Just the sound of Jennifer's voice made Eleanor smile.

"Hi, peeps. You've reached my answering machine. That means I'm either not home or I'm screening my calls and just don't want to talk to *you*. However, you must want to talk to *me* or you wouldn't be calling, so leave me a message. I'll return your call...when I feel like it. Ciao!"

"Hey, girlfriend. What's up? Urg. That's right. You are still at work. My bad." She sighed. "Ah, well, I guess I'll try later...or you could call me. What a novel concept." Eleanor chuckled. "That is, if I'm not on your shit list." She paused, reluctant to give up even this tenuous connection to the outside world. "Okay. I'll talk to you later."

At loose ends and unsure what to do next, she set the receiver back in its cradle. She felt drained and tired and violated. Even though nothing was out of place, she no longer felt safe in her own home. Sitting on the edge of her bed, she put her face in her hands and tried to think, but her mind was blank.

Her body creaked like an old woman's when she stood and looked around her bedroom. Everything was where she had left it, even her glasses. She put them on, walked to the window, and pulled back the curtains to stare out at the fog, its presence no longer comforting. With a sigh, she turned away from the window. Only two more rooms to check.

Dread seized her at the thought. Could someone be hiding in the bathroom? Had they slipped into the living room without her seeing them and hid behind... She chuckled wryly at that thought. The sparse living room furniture left no place to hide, but someone could fit in the front closet. At the thought, her gaze darted to the bedroom closet door. While small, someone could hide in there.

Hesitantly, she approached the closet and stopped. Did she really want to open it without a weapon? A quick scan of the room told her she didn't have a weapon. Offering a silent prayer up to the powers that be, she held her breath and threw the door open.

Her breath escaped with a whoosh. Her shoulders

drooped in relief. Other than her clothes and shoes, the closet was empty.

She shut the door and headed to the bathroom, her back pressed against the wall. The door stood open. Her gaze slid over the toilet, pedestal sink, and claw foot tub. With the shower curtain pushed to the side, no one could hide in the tub.

Scooting the last few steps to the living room, Eleanor paused. She looked back the way she'd come. Nothing. The living room was empty as she suspected it would be. Like all the other rooms, everything rested in its place. The closet next to the front door was the last place to check.

She took a deep breath and left the wall. A spot between her shoulder blades itched as if someone watched her. A glance behind her revealed an empty room. She grasped the doorknob and yanked it open. Winter coats, an umbrella, and boots. Nothing else.

The last of her energy drained from her like blood sucked from a cadaver, but she knew she wasn't done yet. Although she had no proof, she'd feel better if she reported the "break-in" to the authorities. A few more steps brought her to the kitchen where she kept the phone book. She found the number, picked up the phone, and dialed.

"Hello, this is Fresno County Sheriff's Department. How may I help you?" a disembodied woman's voice said.

"I'd like to report a break-in." Eleanor fiddled with phone cord, still unsure how to explain it to them.

"Whom am I speaking to, please?"

"Eleanor. Eleanor Radcliffe."

"Where are you located, Miss Radcliffe?" the woman asked.

"18125 Scotts Valley Road." Her voice shook when she thought about the voice and the break-in again.

"Are you okay, ma'am?" The woman sounded genuinely concerned.

"Yes, just a little unnerved."

"That's to be expected. If you'll give me a cross street, we'll send someone out there as soon as we can."

"That's fine," Eleanor said, although it really wasn't. "The nearest cross street is River and Ashton Ave. Ashton turns into Scotts Valley Rd. I'm about five miles up the road from there on the right side."

"We'll send someone out there as soon as we can, but it will probably be a few hours or tomorrow at the earliest."

"Thank you." She hung up the phone and took a deep breath, trying to dispel some of the tension. She sagged against the kitchen counter and sighed. If she had to, she could get through the night. Hopefully, the sheriff would arrive sooner rather than later.

She sought out the path through the kitchen window, but fog already blanketed the land, and, at that moment, she knew it would be a long, lonely night.

Chapter Two

The ringing of the phone woke Eleanor. Eyes gritty from lack of sleep, she reached for the receiver, groaning in protest. The clock read six a.m. Only one person would dare to call her so early.

"Hello, Jennifer," she mumbled.

"Hey, girlfriend. What's going on? Is everything okay?"

"Other than being woken up at some ungodly hour, why wouldn't it be?" Her gaze fell on the poker lying next to her in bed, a testament to her fear. The bedside lamp lit the room, never turned off from the night before, and she bit her lip to stop the hysterical laughter bubbling up inside of her. What time had the clock read the last time she'd looked at it? 3:30? 4 a.m.?

"Why wouldn't it be?'" Jennifer mimicked her. "I haven't known you for ten years to miss the sound of stifled tears in your voice. So, what's going on?"

Eleanor told her what happened in a few short sentences. She worked pleats in the blue flannel top sheet with her fingers. Each pleat became a little tighter with each word that tumbled out. At the sight of her handiwork, she smoothed the sheets out.

"Did you call the police?" Jennifer demanded.

"Yes," Eleanor said.

"And?"

"They haven't come out yet." She rolled over, threw the covers back, and got out of bed. The brisk air assaulted her senses, and, rubbing her eyes, she searched next to her bed for her worn out slippers, slid them on, slipped her glasses on, and grab the poker off the bed. As she walked by the chair next to the bedroom door, she picked up the bathrobe draped over the back, shrugged it on, and nearly lost the phone and the pokers. The plush material elicited a sigh from her. She needed a cup of coffee. She shuffled through the house, heading toward the kitchen. On the way, she returned the poker to its place next to the fireplace.

"What do you mean 'They haven't come out yet?'" Jennifer nearly screeched.

She smothered a laugh at her friend's reaction, filled a coffee filter, and slid it into its spot. While the incident still bothered her, distance gave her a little more perspective. Well, if not perspective, at least a false sense of security.

"Exactly that. Look. It's not the same as in the city, Jennifer. They'll get here." She filled the coffee pot with water and poured it into the top. "Hopefully not this early."

Jennifer grumbled something too softly for Eleanor to hear and said, "I don't know how you can be so nonchalant about the whole thing."

"Believe me. I wasn't last night, but in the light of day..." She looked out of the window into the darkness and fog. "Okay. Scratch that. With over twelve hours separating me from the occurrence, and your friendly voice, I'm a little better."

An ill-concealed snort echoed through the phone line. "You're fooling yourself."

"No. I made it through the night just fine." *If one didn't count sleeping with my poker and the lights on.* "It was probably just some kids playing a joke."

"Some joke."

Silence filled the line for a moment.

"Eleanor?"

"Yes?"

"Just be careful. You're a long way from nowhere."

Jennifer was really worried. Her voice proclaimed it, but Eleanor had convinced herself that it was a couple of kids playing a joke. She'd report it to the sheriff's department and forget about it.

"I'll be fine," she said.

"Well," her friend replied, "I better go. It's nearly 6:30, and I haven't even showered yet. I'll be late. Man, you have it good, girlfriend. Retired at 35. Now, that's the life. Why you chose Fresno..."

Eleanor laughed. "You'll have to come and visit some time. It's beautiful out here."

"Uh-huh. Sure. I'll talk to you later. Bye, Ellie."

"Ciao, bella."

Eleanor smiled when she set the phone down. Even though Jennifer had woken her, Eleanor didn't mind. It was a wonderful way to begin the day, especially after yesterday. Pouring herself a cup of coffee, she walked into the living room intent on fetching the paper from outside. She swung the door open wide and froze.

The porch light barely penetrated the thick fog. Cold air snaked its way around her bare calves. Goose bumps formed on her legs and spread rapidly over her skin. A shudder shook her entire body. Yesterday morning, she would have fearlessly stepped out, but, now, she hesitated. What if there was someone out there watching her, waiting for her? Even as she argued with herself for being silly, none of her rationale could induce her to venture into the mist. She shut the door and stared at it.

This is silly. Nothing is out there. Despite her protestations, she retreated to the fireplace, set her coffee cup down, and grabbed the poker. Armed, a bit of confidence filled her. She snorted. Who was she kidding? But she hated hiding in the house. Whoever was trying to scare her, she didn't want them to win...at least not without a tussle.

She yanked open the door, the poker raised high. One step out. Nothing happened. Another step, and all remained still. She lowered the poker, beginning to relax. A rustling in the underbrush sent her scuttling backward. As reruns of the day before swirled in her mind's eye, panic tightened its grip upon her, and an involuntary whimper slipped out.

She sprinted back to the house, slammed the door, and slid the bolt home. The poker slipped from her grasp and hit the floor with a dull thud. Adrenaline rushed through her. She dropped down onto the couch, her gaze never straying from the front door, and struggled to slow her erratic breathing and pounding heart. For several minutes, she stared at the door. When nothing happened, the tension slowly seeped out of her, leaving her exhausted.

In search of comfort, she retrieved her coffee cup and took a sip. Her hands were shaking.

* * * *

Two hours later, Eleanor was still sitting on the couch in her flannel pajamas, and her bare feet tucked up beneath her. Her empty coffee cup sat next to her on a couch cushion. She'd been unable to take her gaze off of the front door. No matter what her mind said, she couldn't shake the dread that was slowly building.

Pale morning light filtered through the curtains when she accepted that Jennifer had been right. She was fooling herself. But where could she go? Certainly not back to San Jose. Besides, she didn't want to leave. Up to this point, she had liked it here. She had survived the death of both of her parents. She would make it through this, too. Wouldn't she?

Determination to fight her fear, and not let some prankster scare her away, gained ground. From this moment forward, she refused to be frightened. She wasn't going to spend any more time on this. It was time to make breakfast. With brisk steps, she marched toward the kitchen. Today, she would explore the path she'd seen yesterday. The one that appeared to have set all of this in motion.

Having a plan in mind made her feel better.

* * * *

Eleanor grabbed her coat, pulled on her knit cap and gloves, and stepped out into the mist, determined to re-discover the peace of the first week. As the damp seeped into her skin, she resolved that the quiet of the countryside would, too.

She opened the door and looked straight out the back. From her vantage point, she could clearly see the elusive path. If she walked directly across the creek, the path lay just to the right of the back gate.

Gravel crunched beneath her feet, but she didn't allow the sound to distract her as it normally would. Her gaze remained fixed on the path. She marveled at how she'd missed it the first seven days. Today, she would explore it. With any luck, it would take her mind off of yesterday's fright. The gate squeaked, the noise echoing rudely. Eleanor winced, but her attention never wavered from the break in the trees.

Just across the creek, the path beckoned. She looked down and nimbly hopped from one rock to the next until she reached the bank. Once safely on the other side, she looked up and gasped.

A tall, slender man holding a cowboy hat in one hand and leading a horse with the other stared back at her. He stood on the path. Not a sound had announced his arrival. Shivers ran down her spine. Goose bumps trailed in their wake. Where had he come from? Beyond him, the path stretched into the oak forest.

"I'm sorry to disturb you, but I saw you stepping out for a walk and I thought I would introduce myself. If now is a bad time..."

"No," Eleanor shook her head, "it's all right." But it wasn't all right. His sudden appearance rattled her. However, she'd never let him know it. "I was just going to explore that path you're standing on."

She took in his appearance, detailing everything in case she needed to report him to the police. Even the country had weirdoes inhabiting it. Wavy brown hair framed a rugged face. His hair looked so soft and silky that Eleanor's original intention became lost in a sudden tingle of awareness. She itched to sink her hands into it even as her survival instinct called her a fool. A prickle of desire spread through her. Her gaze slipped past his tawny one, over his high cheekbones, his smiling lips, and square jaw. Self-conscious, she couldn't meet his eyes and looked at the ground instead.

The silence stretched between them. She shifted, unsure what to say. She looked back up at his face. He watched her intently. The heat of embarrassment crept up her neck and filled her cheeks. She only hoped he couldn't read her jumpiness or recognize the rush of desire that surged through her when their gazes met.

The man's smile seemed innocuous. "I've been meaning to stop by, but we've been busy at the ranch. Then I saw you walking through the woods the other day, and I thought I might catch you out here again sometime." He studied Eleanor's face. "I thought that it was very un-neighborly of me not to come over to say 'hello'."

A sliver of unease wormed its way into Eleanor's thoughts.

"You saw me in the woods?" Her voice rose, and she took a breath before continuing. "But the closest house is five miles away."

He chuckled, a deep, rumbling sound that rolled over her and sent a quiver of awareness dancing down her spine. "Not quite five. More like one mile." He smiled at her. "I forget how living this far out can be a bit disconcerting at first. I live in that house beyond the woods. I often ride my horse out this way looking for stray cattle. They like to follow the creek." He set his hat on his head and held out his gloved hand to help her up onto solid ground. "I'm Michael Stevens. My brothers and I run the family ranch. We own most of the property just to the south of you as well as east and west."

Eleanor looked at the leather-covered hand for a moment before taking it and stepped up onto the bank. An electrical charge zipped between them, and she smothered the urge to pull farther away. *Where had this man come from?*

"Eleanor Radcliffe. I hope you don't mind me walking on your property. I know I'm trespassing, but..."

Michael shrugged. "We don't mind, but I thought I should warn you. It's easy to lose your bearings and get lost out here, especially in the fog. And unlike the city, we have wild animals. Coyotes will leave you alone for the most part, but packs of wild dogs and cougars may not. Although they are less likely to bother me on my horse, I carry a shotgun just in case. We try to keep the packs of dogs off our property, but, sometimes, they sneak past us, and we don't catch them for a few days."

Great. One more thing to worry about. Not only do the police never arrive to find out if you are still alive after a break-in, but I could be killed by wild animals.

"So, I shouldn't take walks?"

"Not alone, at least."

Disappointment flowed through her. Her plan to explore the path that he stood on floated away like the mist.

"I suppose I'll just stay in my garden."

"That would be safer...unless you'd like company." A flush spread across his high cheekbones.

She smiled, relief spreading through her. He appeared as uncomfortable as she, but friendly. Perhaps she was being too hasty in thinking he might be dangerous. Besides, to have such a handsome man attracted to her was flattering, and rare. It wasn't like she was a super model. Heck, she wasn't even a catalog model. With unremarkable brown hair, plain features, and a plump body, she didn't inflame men with unbridled lust, let alone have them lining up to proclaim their undying love for her. Her silvery gray eyes were her one saving grace, although not enough to overcome everything else, if one could see them past the glasses, that was.

His horse jerked on the reins, and Michael looked over his shoulder, murmuring gently to it. Eleanor took the opportunity to survey the rest of him. Even through his bulky sheepskin jacket, he appeared well built. His thighs looked muscular under the jeans that hugged a slim waist.

"That would be lovely. I've spent the last week alone which, although a nice change, is growing a bit old," she said, knowing an answer was required of her.

"Would you like to see the path now?" he asked.

"I..." Eleanor looked behind her, her tan house nearly blending in with a drifting patch of fog except for the dark windows. Empty. The house was empty...at least, the last time she had checked it was. Of course, they may, or may not, be in it now. She could return to her house and be alone or join Michael. Decision made, she turned back to him and smiled.

"Thank you," she said. "I'd love to."

His golden gaze sparkled with appreciation, and he smiled back. "Come on, Butte," he said, turning his horse around to face the path. "The lady wants to see some of our land." He held his hand out to her.

Unaccustomed to a man showing such courtesy, she hesitated, but the warm look in his eyes and his non-threatening stance convinced her that she was safe. She sensed he would allow her to take the lead. A feeling of power rolled through her. With her fear behind her, other emotions emerged, emotions she'd never experienced before.

She sneaked a look at his profile. His stubble shadow, slightly crooked nose, and strong chin didn't classify him as traditionally handsome, but his lips looked soft, kissable, and laugh lines etched the skin around his eyes. Not a Greek god, but pretty damn close. A one-night stand had never fit her personality before, but she'd consider it with him.

What was she thinking? She'd just met this man, and she was already fantasizing about him. Too much time alone and feeling giddy with just a little bit of non-threatening human contact. That was it.

"So," she started, searching for something to say. "Have you lived here long?"

The skin around his eyes crinkled with his amusement. He seemed to be chuckling inwardly, although he didn't let it show in his voice. "All my life."

"You've never lived anywhere else?" She couldn't fathom living her entire life in one place. "Not even for college?"

"Nope." He looked down at her, his eyes sparkling with mirth. "I never saw a reason to. I've spent my entire life ranching, and I love this land. Look around you."

Tall oak trees dotted the rolling hills. Green patches of grass interspersed with brown. Some of the grasses had silver heads with green new growth at the bottom. The occasional outcropping of granite jutted up from the trees and grass. Shrouded in silvery mist, the land felt like it belonged to another world, one where magic and reality coexisted. She shook her head at the thought.

Michael said, "Why would I leave this?"

She nodded in agreement.

They walked in silence, soaking in the serenity. His hand warmed hers even through their gloves, and peace returned to Eleanor. She stopped and turned to thank him. Their gazes met. Banked desire flickered in the depths of his eyes, eliciting a response from deep within her. Her reaction excited and scared her. Instinctively, she knew it was too soon and could be a reaction to yesterday's event. No, if anything came of this chance meeting, she wanted to take it nice and slow.

She turned toward home, ignoring his desire and the question in his eyes. "It's lovely out here, but cold."

He nodded and turned with her. Butte followed behind him.

At the creek, he stopped. "Well, I should get going. I have a few chores to do. Just give me a call whenever you feel the desire to go walking. If I can, I'll come."

"You're not going to come in?" she asked, unable to hide her disappointment.

He shook his head. "No, ma'am. Not now. I have stayed longer than I should have. But I'll be back. I promise."

"When?" She hated sounding like a clingy female, but a fear that she wouldn't see him again rushed over her.

"All you have to do is call," he replied. He stepped back and mounted his horse.

"Thank you." Even to her ears, it sounded inane, but she didn't want him to go just yet.

"It's my pleasure," he said and turned Butte onto the path.

"Good bye." Her voice came out more breathy than she intended. Heat prickled up her neck and cheeks.

He looked over his shoulder at her. "Good bye."

His gaze promised pleasure. Pleasure she suddenly wanted more than anything. She watched him ride away and ground her teeth to keep from calling after him. Only when he was no longer in sight, did Eleanor realize that she didn't have his phone number.

Chapter Three

The house was quiet when she returned. Nothing out of place. No windows or doors stood open. She could almost believe last night had never happened.

The doorbell rang, sending her pulse racing faster than a greyhound. Could it be Michael? She drew in a deep breath and walked briskly to the door, almost throwing it open. Disappointment filled her at the sight of a chest clad in tan and sporting a sheriff's badge instead of soft flannel and leather.

She had to tip her head back to see his face. The somber expression on the handsome face gave nothing away.

"Miss Radcliffe? I'm Officer Rodney Tyler." Intense brown eyes studied her.

Eleanor shook his hand. Memories of her fear from the day before came rushing back.

"May I come in?"

"Uh, sure." She stepped back to give him room to enter. Cold air wrapped its arms around her. A shiver shimmied down her back, and she quickly shut the door. The fog's embrace had lost its allure.

He scanned the sparsely furnished living room, stopping on her dinosaur of a television. He didn't even raise an eyebrow. "You reported a break in? Was anything taken?"

"No. I..." Embarrassment heated her cheeks. How could she explain what had happened without sounding psycho? She licked her lips, looked down at her feet, and grimaced. Mud covered her sturdy hiking boots. She'd obviously just been out walking. Would he question her story more because of it?

A warm hand rested briefly on her shoulder. She jumped, startled. Their gazes met. For the second time that day, she read interest in a man's eyes. She, who barely made a ripple when she walked through a room, had two very good-looking men interested. The sensation was heady. Blushing, she moved to the couch and sat down. When she faced him again, she felt more in control.

"I don't know how to explain this without sounding like a crackpot, but yesterday I was sitting at my kitchen table when I saw a figure standing out in the fog..." She told him what happened.

He remained silent through the whole recitation, making her nerves jump. Did he believe her or was he merely humoring her?

"Does anyone else have a key?" Officer Tyler asked.

"Not that I'm aware of. I bought this house over a month ago, but only moved in last week. When I moved in, it was vacant."

"Are you certain you didn't open the window?"

"In the middle of winter?"

"I have to ask to rule out all of the possibilities," he replied. He once again scanned the living room. "Do you mind if I take a look around? Maybe you missed something." He closed his notebook and strode toward the front door.

"Do you want to see the bedroom window?" Heat flooded her cheeks. That hadn't come out the way she meant it. Would he think it was an invitation? His lack of response told her it was only in her mind. She sighed in relief and continued. "I didn't see anything that would suggest someone had forced it, but I don't have much experience with this kind of thing."

He shook his head. "Let me look around outside first. I'll check inside later."

She followed him to the door and watched him through her window. He pulled his radio out and started to talk to someone the second he stepped out of earshot. She sensed that he didn't believe her. Heck! She had a hard time believing it and she'd lived through it.

"He's a fool," a voice whispered.

The hair on the back of her neck stood on end. Her heart pounding an uneven tattoo, she turned to look behind her, afraid of what she may, or may not, see. The room was empty, but she heard the kitchen door slam. Pulling open the front door, she ran outside to the officer.

"It happened again." Her breath came in short gasps. "Someone was in my house. They went out the back."

"Stay here," he ordered and rushed into the house.

She looked around and scuttled after him. Nothing could induce her to stand outside in the cold, with the fog hanging in the distance, alone. He moved quickly through the house with Eleanor on his heels. He stopped so abruptly in the kitchen that she bumped into his back. The look he gave her made her insides churn, but fear of the unknown kept her glued to his side.

Peeking around his shoulder, she saw two small muddy footprints on the floor about the size of an eight- or nine-year-old child. He crossed to the backdoor and looked out the window. She knew he wouldn't see anything.

"I called the station," he began, but stopped. Concern filled his eyes.

"I know. I saw you on your radio. I figured you were calling in about the crazy lady."

He shook his head and appeared hesitant to continue. "What do you know about this house?"

"Only that I love it. Why?" A very bad feeling stole over her, similar to how she felt right before her mother told her she had cancer.

"Apparently, your house is a favorite place for neighborhood kids to pull pranks. At least, that is the best we can figure." He took in the cozy kitchen before he turned back to her. "You've been here a week?"

She nodded, wondering how the sheriff's department could call this a neighborhood kid's prank, especially after seeing the small bare footprints. What child would run around in the middle of winter without shoes? What mother would let them? And how could there be neighborhood kids without a neighborhood? "Yesterday was exactly a week."

"It fits the pattern. That's when the pranks begin. Most of the pranks are harmless."

"Most?" she interrupted.

"Yes. On occasion, things are destroyed. In any case, we've been unable to catch them. The best I can do is write down another report and advise you to get to know your neighbors."

"That's it?" she asked. This was all he was going to do?

"Miss Radcliffe, I wish I could do more for you. Unfortunately, beyond setting up camp, which I am not allowed to do, it's the best I can do. However," he pulled out a card, quickly jotted something down on the back, and handed it to her, "when...uh, if this happens again, call me directly. Or just call me if you feel the need...for anything." His radio squawked. "Officer Tyler here," he answered. "I'm sorry. I have to go." He strode across the yard to his parked patrol car, climbed in, and started the engine.

Stunned by his abrupt exit, she stared after him. She finally found her voice as she watched his car pull out of the driveway. "What about my bedroom?" she asked to the air. With his card in her hand, she wanted to cry then throw something and cry some more. Useless. Absolutely useless. She had expected to feel safer after talking to a sheriff. Instead, she felt even more vulnerable. She looked at the back of the card. 555-0892 – home. Officer Rodney Tyler.

Where was Michael when she needed him? And how did she know he could help her?

* * * *

The fog was creeping in later that afternoon when another knock sounded on her front door. Not sure whether she wanted to open it or not, Eleanor dragged herself from her Sudoku puzzle and went to answer it.

A slim woman holding a plate of cookies smiled at her from her doorstep. The woman handed her the treats and glided past her.

"Hello. I'm Lily Johanson, one of your neighbors." The woman chuckled. "Although, technically, we're not neighbors if you consider the distance between our houses." Her hazel eyes alight with amusement, she shook Eleanor's hand and turned to survey her barely furnished living room. "I take it you are a minimalist decorator."

Eleanor opened her mouth to speak, but Lily was already moving toward the kitchen.

"I like that. So many people clutter their houses with 'dust collectors', myself included. If I could just bring myself to part with some of my crap, my house would be so much cleaner." She sighed theatrically, sitting down in one of the kitchen chairs. "Alas, I cannot. I am always afraid of

21

offending whoever gave me that ghastly trinket. You know, I once received a candle in the shape of a Chihuahua for Christmas. Do you know what I did with it?"

Not sure how to answer, Eleanor shook her head.

"It sits in a place of honor on my mantle." The woman rolled her eyes. "That's right. Five years later, and I still have it in my house. Of course, my children love it, but..." She stopped mid-sentence. "Well, I didn't come here to spill my life story. I came here to meet you and welcome you to our little neighborhood and to offer anything I can in the way of help."

Again, a response eluded Eleanor. The woman was like a whirling dervish. Her melodious voice seemed out of place with the bubbly woman's personality. And while the woman seemed very nice, Eleanor just wasn't accustomed to such friendliness from neighbors.

"Help?" Eleanor finally gasped out.

"Oh, yes. You arrived what—a week ago—well, surely you can't be done unpacking yet." The stream of words stopped abruptly as Lily inspected the room again. "I take that back. You're done, aren't you?"

It wasn't a question, but Eleanor nodded anyway.

"Anyway, I noticed that you seem to stay home a great deal. Being a stay-at-home mom, I know what it can be like to be tied to your house with no human interaction— well, I have my children, but it's not the same as having adult conversation, you know. And with my husband being a rancher, I see him late in the evenings. So, maybe this is for my benefit. In any case, this place has a history of driving its owners away. The sheriff's department claims it's neighborhood kids, but I don't believe it. We have similar activity at our farm, but not nearly like here, and I can tell you, I know the neighborhood kids. They are more interested in escaping the area and visiting the mall in Clovis than they are in terrorizing neighbors."

Eleanor didn't want to hear this. Neighborhood kids she could deal with.

"So, I just wanted to let you know... What did you say your name was?"

"Eleanor. Eleanor Radcliffe," she replied.

"What a lovely name! I always wanted a regal name like that." She laughed again. "I'm sorry. I'm off topic. I have a tendency to follow tangents. In any case, I came to offer our house should you need a place to stay some night."

"Will I need one?"

"Well..." For the first time since her visit, Lily hesitated. "Maybe not. But it's always nice to know you have somewhere to turn."

"Uh, okay." Eleanor rose and walked over to the sink. "I was just about to make myself a cup of coffee. Would you like one?"

"No, thank you," Lily said, standing. "I have to get back to the house before the kids come home from school. I just came by to say 'hello' and offer our hospitality, should you need it."

Eleanor escorted her to the door, unsure whether she'd just made a friend, or Lily had come over to gain her measure. The whole exchange was rather odd. But then, since yesterday, the world she lived in had become rather odd.

Chapter Four

For the second morning in a row, Eleanor rose early. This time, it wasn't her friend Jennifer calling, but someone ringing the doorbell. She groaned, rolled over, and looked at the clock. Seven a.m. Couldn't they bother her at a decent hour? Like nine? Ten? After another sleepless night, where nothing happened—thank goodness—she wanted to sleep until noon.

Reluctantly, she sat up, her eyes gritty with sleep, crossed to the window, and peeked out. Her heart pounded. Michael stood, hat in hand, at the front door. Two horses waited patiently behind him, stomping their feet. White puffs of steam hung before the horses' faces where warm breath met cold air.

Energy zipped through her, and the tiredness that had gripped her moments before slipped away. Rushing to the closet, she threw off her nightclothes, shivering in the cool air, and donned some jeans, a turtleneck, a sweater, thick socks, and her sturdy walking boots. If she'd learned one thing since moving to Fresno, the fog seeped into everything. Better to layer and look bulky than freeze, especially if he intended to take her riding. She grabbed her glasses and put them on.

She returned to the window, knocking on it. He looked toward her and smiled. She waved and gestured for him to wait a few more minutes. He nodded. She ran to the bathroom, quickly brushed her teeth, pulled a brush through her hair, and grimaced at her reflection. She usually liked her curly hair, unless it was humid. Humidity made her hair frizzy and unmanageable. No amount of brushing seemed to tame it. Mixed with the circles under her eyes, against her olive complexion, and she was *so attractive*. But she didn't have time for makeup, nor did she think any amount would improve her haggard appearance. Only sleep would do that, and she wasn't going to get anymore this morning. Not that she was complaining. She'd take a ride with Michael over sleep any time.

Her heart fluttered in anticipation, her steps quickening as she strode to open the front door. She gave him her biggest smile, and her breath hitched. No one in her old life would believe her if she told them how attractive a man in a padded plaid flannel shirt, wearing a cowboy hat, could be. Of course, he could wear a pink tutu and still look delicious.

He'd look even better naked.

She looked at the ground to hide the heat suffusing her cheeks.

He cleared his throat, and their gazes met. His sparkled with amusement and interest. Her blush deepened.

She opened her mouth to say something, hoping he wouldn't notice her embarrassment, and they started speaking at the same time.

"I—" Her voice trailed off at the sound of his voice.

"I—" He stopped and chuckled. "You first."

"No. That's all right. You go." The words rushed out of her. His chuckle poured over her like semi-sweet chocolate syrup on vanilla ice cream, and her mind turned to mush as the sound of his laughter surrounded her. His golden gaze was the butterscotch. Now all she needed was the banana, and she'd be set.

"I thought you might like to go riding after our discussion yesterday. You appeared to be interested in viewing the countryside. There's no better way to see it than on the back of a horse."

Provided she could concentrate on their surroundings and not her lust... that was. Unable to speak, she nodded.

"You may want to grab your jacket. The fog is colder than it first appears."

She nodded yet again. Her mouth went dry. The prospect of spending a few hours with him set her pulse to racing. A thrill zipped through her. She turned away from him and repressed the urge to skip through the house to the kitchen to retrieve her jacket, hat, and scarf that hung on pegs next to her backdoor. A huge grin spread across her face. She knew if she saw herself in the mirror, she'd look like a dopey fool, but damn! It felt good to have such an attractive man want her even at her worst.

A few minutes later, she locked the front door, her keys safely in her coat pocket, and stepped outside. Michael held the reins in his hands. The horses were stamping their feet, trying to keep warm.

"Do you know how to ride?" he asked.

"Not well, but I'm game."

"Then let me give you a brief lesson. Never approach a horse from behind, always mount a horse from their left side, and never let them know you're scared. Of course, you don't have to worry about that with Old Sally here." He patted the buff-colored horse standing next to Butte.

"Sally?" What an absurd name for a horse.

He grinned. "Yup. Short for Salamander. You'd never guess it, but Sally loves the water. She loves to swim and is nearly amphibious for a horse. Never had to urge her across a stream to chase wayward cattle. But don't worry. The creek's not high enough this time of year, and even if she is tempted, she won't jump in the water with you on her back. When she was younger, now that's another story."

Great. A horse that likes water.

"Other than that one trait, Sally's very gentle. You needn't worry about her taking off or startling easily." He offered her his hand. "Let me help you up."

She put her hand in his and suppressed the sudden surge of desire. She moved quickly to the horse. Any more of this and she'd be a mindless bimbo and throw herself at him. She placed her foot in the stirrup and grasped the saddle horn, preparing to swing her leg over the back of the horse. The feel of his warm hand on her bottom startled her so much she nearly fell back into him. Her grip tightened on the saddle horn. He pushed, and she pulled herself up. She'd forgotten how hard it was to mount a horse.

"Thank you," she murmured.

He rested his hand on her leg, the heat sending shivers through her. "Do you know how to turn the horse, hold the reins, or would you be more comfortable riding behind me?"

"Uh..." The thought of sitting behind him, her arms wrapped around him, for an hour or two was a little too much for her. She knew her limit. Besides, she barely knew him, making the strength of her desire rather frightening.

And she didn't want to appear like a total ignorant-of-the-country city slicker. The more distance she had from him, the better. "I think I'll be okay."

"Let me show you how to hold the reins then. You won't be going anywhere with that death grip."

After a few more instructions, he mounted Butte, and they set off at a slow walk. Unaccustomed to the rocking motion of Sally's gait, Eleanor gripped the horse tightly with her legs. Sally sped up to a trot. Eleanor grabbed the saddle horn and squeezed harder. Sally's speed increased.

Panicked, Eleanor looked over at Michael who kept pace with her, his eyes twinkling. "I thought you said she was gentle."

"She is, but you've told her you want to go faster. Relax your legs and pull back on the reins. She'll slow down again." He reached over and grabbed the reins, bringing Sally to a stop. "Are you sure you don't want to ride behind me?"

Reluctantly, she relaxed and nodded. "I can do this. I just need practice."

"Obviously." Humor laced his voice, but he managed to keep a straight face.

"I'm glad you think this is funny." She glared at him, but couldn't stop her answering grin. Here she was trying to impress him, and she ended up looking like a goober. Typical. Her horse jerked forward, jolting her out of her thoughts. Once again, she found herself gripping the horn.

A chuckle drifted in the air behind her followed by an amused voice. "Relax your legs. Remember, gripping tight will make her move faster."

A vision of her legs wrapped around him filled her head. Would he move faster if she gripped him tightly? She looked away, unable to meet his gaze. He guided his horse to the back of her property, and she followed him, concentrating on staying atop the horse. They rode along the creek. The rustle of leaves and the muffled clop of the horse's hooves filled the silence.

He motioned for her to ride abreast of him and pointed to a tree. "See this tree?"

She nodded.

"It's a Valley oak. They only grow in the San Joaquin

Valley and can live 300 or more years. Some historical accounts claim that the Valley oaks covered every inch of the San Joaquin Valley from the Sierra Nevada range to the mountains sixty or so miles west of us. There are those who say these oaks are endangered. Looking around us, you'd never think it possible. The blue jays stay busy planting the acorns, ensuring there will be many more oaks for generations to come. Of course, if the builders keep developing the land the way they have these past couple of years, the oaks could disappear." Sadness filled his eyes. "Even in the winter when their branches are bare, these are majestic trees. It would be a tragedy to lose them."

He pulled his horse to a stop next to one of the trees and rested his hand on its trunk. He seemed to draw strength from the tree, and she thought she heard the tree sigh.

His obvious passion and attachment for his surroundings stirred a yearning deep inside of her. What would it feel like to be that connected to the land?

Their gazes met, and he smiled. "There are many secrets out here. Secrets only Mother Nature can tell you if you'll listen. However, I'm not Mother Nature." A self-deprecating grin spread across his face, his eyes twinkling as if he laughed at himself. "All these long, solitary hours in the saddle with nothing but cattle for company can get to a man."

Eleanor laughed and shook her head. "No. Don't apologize. I think your reverence for the land is wonderful. So few share it. They don't see the land for more than what they can grasp from it." She surveyed the countryside, breathing in the crisp, winter air. "I fell in love with it the moment I saw it. Now if only..." She nearly confided in him about her problems at the house. Looking through the trees, she tried to hide her discomfort. It was enough that the police officer thought she was whacked. She didn't want Michael to think so, too.

The sound of fluttering wings and a tap-tapping drew her attention. Up in the tree, a black and white bird with a red cap on its head struck its beak against the trunk. She marveled at the speed with which the woodpecker hammered on the tree. A drummer would envy the bird's percussive abilities.

"One of the many native birds, the Acorn woodpecker."

For the next few hours, she listened with rapt attention. Awed by his knowledge of the native flora and fauna, she wondered how she'd lived for so long in San Jose and never known that much about the plants and birds of the region. Had she been that self-involved? Shaking her head, she decided that now was not the time to beat herself up over the past. In the privacy of her own room, she could do that. Right now, enjoying Michael's company ranked much higher on her list of priorities.

Reluctantly, they turned their horses back toward the house, the sound of the horses' hooves muffled in the fallen leaves. Eleanor drew the cold air into her lungs and marveled at the peace and contentment that filled her. This was what she had sought when she moved here. What she had found until only a few days past and the "incidents" started.

She turned to Michael. He sat erect in his saddle, his face in profile showing a bump in the middle of his nose she hadn't noticed before. She wondered how that had happened. Had he broken his nose during a fall while chasing down cattle?

He turned to face her and smiled. An answering smile spread across her face, and a voice whispered to her heart. Like a morning glory opening for the sun, joy burst in her chest, and she gasped at the sensation. Without a word, they reached out and touched hands. The horses slowed to a halt only a few inches apart.

Banked desire turned his eyes the color of molten gold. An answering need roared to life within her. A question formed in his eyes, and, unconsciously, she answered it, leaning toward him and lifting her lips to meet his. His lips captured hers. Cold and moist collided with the hot air of their breath as their mouths opened to taste one another.

Surrendering to the rampant yearning, Eleanor released his hand and slid hers up and into his hair. Unable to feel its texture through her gloves, she pulled them off. They fell to the ground. The silky texture of his hair contrasted sharply with his rough stubble. She squirmed in the saddle, and Sally nickered in protest.

Their lips parted, and breathless laughter filled the air.

"We might be safer on the ground," Michael said, dismounting.

"Oh, I don't know. I think I might be safer on the horse." Chuckling, she stared down at him.

He proffered his hand. She studied it. Her rash actions sent questions shooting through her mind. What was she doing? She didn't know this man very well. How did she know she could trust him? She didn't, but she wanted to take a chance. One more kiss wouldn't hurt... Would it?

Decision made, she slipped off the horse and nearly fell over, her legs wobbling from too long in the saddle. His arms caught fast around her, and she leaned into him, using her unsteady legs as an excuse to slip her arms around him. Unable to resist, she flicked her tongue out to taste the heated skin that peeked out from his jacket. Electricity zinged through her, and she shuddered.

A ragged moan escaped him, and he buried his hands deep in her hair. "Eleanor."

Passion warred with warning in his tone, fanning her desire, enticing her to see how far she could push him. She reached for the buttons on his jacket, but one of the horses pawed the ground and signaled its impatience.

Michael drew back with a rueful smile. "Butte is right. This isn't the place for this." He cupped her cheek, his thumb gently stroking it. The look in his eyes told her he didn't want to stop any more than she wanted him to. "Don't look at me like that."

"Like what?"

"Like I ate your last piece of chocolate." He grinned and assisted her onto Sally's back.

She smiled down at him. "Now, those are fightin' words, mister. Keep your paws off my chocolate."

He pulled himself onto Butte, swinging his leg over, and winked at her. "I don't play fair, miss, so I'd be careful if I were you."

Laughter spilled out of her, tinkling gaily in the cold air.

The smile remained firmly on her face the rest of the way home.

Chapter Five

The rest of the day passed slowly. Now that she could no longer explore the countryside alone, she sat at the table in the breakfast nook and stared out the window, daydreaming about her neighbor. She replayed their passionate embrace over and over again. Part of her couldn't believe her unfettered response, but another part of her reveled in her spontaneous action. If the horses hadn't shifted, she knew that the dead leaves would have been their carpet and the barren branches their ceiling. She would have returned home with leaves in her hair and wet clothes, but it would have been worth it.

Small mewing sounds escaped her, and she wiggled on her seat. For the first time in her thirty-five years, she felt the urge to masturbate. With both of her parents gone and no siblings, she didn't have anyone to disapprove of her actions. Not that she would have told them, but she'd always felt they would know if she took care of her own needs.

And she had needs. Needs that simmered below the surface, occasionally awakened by the touch or the glance of a boyfriend.

The fog crept forward as she watched and fantasized. It swallowed her back gate first then the farthest end of her garden. By nightfall, the fog embraced the house in its cold, slippery grasp. Water dripped off the eaves, and small droplets formed on the windows. The droplets coagulated into shapes, multiplying and joining together. The shapes became more and more distinct until she recognized them.

Pushing away from the table, Eleanor turned her back on the image of herself laughing up at Michael, denying what she saw. It was her imagination working overtime again. She'd spent most of the day cooped up in the house, thoughts of Michael her only entertainment. That she would see herself and him in the condensation on the window didn't surprise her.

She looked at the clock over the stove and stood. Where had the time gone? How had she spent four hours daydreaming?

Because the subject was oh so delectable. However delectable his image was, it wouldn't fill her grumbling belly.

Opening the refrigerator, Eleanor stared at its contents. Nothing appealed to her. For the first time since moving out here, she yearned for someone else's company. She yearned for one specific person's company: Michael's, but he wasn't here and wouldn't be until tomorrow or the next day or maybe not at all. Why hadn't she thought of asking for his number before he disappeared into the fog? Because she was twitter-pated and aching with need. Her mind wouldn't function properly.

She refused to let him dominate her thoughts for the rest of the night. Grilled cheese and vegetable soup sounded perfect for such a cold, soggy night. Determined to focus on anything but him and all the nonsense, she set to work making dinner.

But the "nonsense" wouldn't go away. It haunted her while she fixed dinner. It followed her when she sat down to watch a little television to accompany her dinner. It chased her into the kitchen and teased her as she rinsed the dishes and put them away. She couldn't escape the images of her and Michael locked in a passionate embrace.

Why did he affect her so? He was a handsome man, although not the best looking she'd ever seen, but he mesmerized her, his gaze whispered of secret pleasures. And his voice... His voice was enough to make her blood pulse.

"Oh, Michael, why didn't I get your phone number?" she spoke aloud to the empty room.

"Eleanor."

She shivered. Were her thoughts so powerful as to conjure his voice?

"Eleanor..." the voice said a little louder.

"Michael?" Her body tingled at the thought of seeing him, kissing him, again. She scanned the room. It was empty. Although she knew he couldn't possibly be in her house, disappointment filled her.

"Eleanor..."

The whisper brushed her ear, fanning the fire she'd kept banked all day with her fantasizing. She spun, but no one was behind her. Her heart thudded in her chest. What was happening to her? Was she losing her mind?

"I'm right here, Eleanor. Open your mind. I'm standing behind you."

Fear and excitement zipped through her. Was it possible? Was he in her house? But how? *No. It's not possible,* her rational mind answered. *Go to bed.* She glanced at the clock. It was only eight o'clock and too early for bed. If she tried, she would toss and turn for at least an hour. Reading wouldn't work, and watching TV was not an option either.

She sighed. Leaving her living room, she walked into her bathroom and turned the water on, adding a cupful of rose-scented bath bubbles, then crossed the hall to her bedroom and grabbed her pink, fluffy bathrobe, her underwear, and flannel pajamas. While the tub filled, Eleanor stared at herself in the bathroom mirror, not really seeing her reflection.

Her heart ached with the loneliness resulting from her mother's death. Surely that would explain her fixation on Michael, the voices, and the faces in the windows. It had to be. The only other option was that she was insane. She sincerely hoped it was the first.

Water spilled over the side of the tub, bringing Eleanor out of her reverie.

"Damn," she muttered, quickly turning the spigot off and opening the drain to let some water out before doffing her clothes and climbing in.

A sigh escaped her as the heat of the water seeped into her tense muscles, relaxing her. She hummed tunelessly to herself, languidly running the washcloth up and down her arms, over her breasts, down her stomach, and all the way down the length of her long legs. After bathing her feet, she leaned back against the cool tub and rested her head on the pillow she kept there. Closing her eyes, she allowed her mind to wander to that afternoon. Once again, Michael filled her mind. The images were so strong she could smell his scent and feel his lips on hers.

Strong hands cupped her breasts, and she pushed into them. The tingling sensation spread from her nipples all the way down to her nether regions. A bare, hairy leg brushed against hers. Her toes curled, and she rubbed her feet against the leg. At the contact, her eyes flew open. Michael stood above her in all his naked glory. The light fur on his chest trailed down his taut stomach in a narrow line, drawing her to his cock. His erection stoked the fever in her blood. She tried to speak, but he was so beautiful the words wouldn't pass her open lips.

His tawny gaze turned fiery with desire, and he smiled a devastating smile that spoke of carnal pleasures. "Is there room for me in here?"

She nodded, her mind paralyzed for a moment. All of her attention was focused on his magnificent frame.

"Sit up and move forward," he commanded.

She complied without thought. He slid into the tub behind her, his legs cupping her. His hard on jerked when it came in contact with her bare skin, evoking a response from deep inside of her.

"It's a tight fit." He picked up the soap and began lathering her up.

"I'm clean," she murmured. Anticipation turned her insides to molten lava.

"Not clean enough." His breath puffed gently in her ear and sent chills skipping along her nerve endings. Carefully replacing the soap, he started massaging her shoulders and neck.

She moaned and dropped her head back onto his shoulder. Large hands slid down her arms, massaging as they went. His lips nibbled on her ear, and his uneven breath blew gently on her cheek.

She moved to face him, and his hands cupped her breasts and gently flicked her nipples, bringing them to hard buds.

He whispered, "No. Not yet. I'm not done."

With his fingers, he traced a path down her stomach to her slick sheath. He slipped a finger inside and groaned his approval. His hips lifted as if they were as impatient as he. He stroked her with his finger, his hips moving in concert with them, until she couldn't think of anything but his touch. At the first signs of her muscles contracting, he pulled her up and pushed into her from behind.

Her eyes flew open in surprise, but she didn't protest. Instead, she shoved back against him and sought to seat him deeper. The scent of their lovemaking swirled around her, teased her. An animalistic grunt of gratification escaped him, and he rubbed her clit, urging her onward. Just when she felt her body could take no more, waves of intense bliss rolled over her, rocking her body with their force. He pulsed inside of her.

A deep contentment settled over her as he kissed her cheek lightly; he caressed her lazily now. She relaxed into his embrace and drifted to sleep.

The cool porcelain of the bathtub and water intruded upon her slumber. Slowly, she became aware of her surroundings. Silence wrapped its arms around her, broken only by her even breathing. Her eyes popped open. She was alone. No sign of Michael anywhere.

Relief tinged with regret colored her sigh. It had been a dream. A very vivid dream, but a dream nonetheless. Wearily, she stood, picked up her towel, and let out the water. Blindly, she stared at the water as it was sucked down the drain. Her gaze zeroed in on something that looked out of place.

There, in the water stark against the remaining suds, was a strand of short, wavy brown hair.

Unable to believe her eyes and overcome by the events of the past weeks, Eleanor dropped down onto the toilet seat cover and cried. She couldn't ignore it anymore. Something was very wrong with this house, with her.

Chapter Six

Two days passed. Not another soul came to visit her, and Eleanor wondered if she had imagined everything, if her mind was playing tricks on her due to her long periods of solitude and grief over her mother's death. Watching someone lose her life essence in a painful, slow descent into nothingness stole a portion of that person's soul, too. Had it sapped some of her sanity?

She shook her head. No. Michael lived beyond her dreams. Their passionate kiss of two days past still sent electrical currents racing through her nerve endings. And the bathtub scene... She flushed at the memory of the dream. Best not to think about it. As for Officer Tyler, he was real. His card proved his existence. And, surely, the empty plate, once filled with Lily's cookies that now sat on her counter waiting for her to return it, could only mean Lily was part of this world and not a dream.

Against her better judgment, Eleanor hoped that Michael would drop by.

A sigh escaped her. It figured. She likes a guy, he likes her—or so it would seem from his kisses—then he disappears, and she spends her days creating fantasies out of thin air and pining for him. She should just call Officer Tyler. At least she had his phone number.

Eleanor shook her head, denying the urge. Maybe later. Right now, she would rather procrastinate and finish the Sudoku puzzle. She might not solve it, but it wouldn't reject her.

A few hours later, Eleanor looked up from washing the dinner dishes and gasped. A face smiled back at her in the condensation. Her heart pounding, she shook her head to dispel the image, but it didn't work. Her mother used to tell her that her imagination rivaled that of ten people combined. She had always taken it as a compliment. Now, she wondered. Leaning closer for a better look, she studied the face. It was really quite defined. Had the mouth twitched? She jumped back, fighting the urge to run. Lily's voice echoed in her mind.

Impossible. "Get a grip, Eleanor."

Her voice echoed in the quiet house, mocking her. She didn't believe in ghosts. She just needed some human companionship besides her imagination.

Putting the towel in its place under the sink, she turned her back on the window, the mist, and the face, flipped the switch on the radio to "on", grabbed her book, and walked into the living room to read. A fire crackled in the fireplace. Its flames leaped and danced, pulling her attention away from her book.

With a sigh, she set the book down in disgust and turned off the radio. Maybe television would relieve the feeling that she was being watched. She snorted. She doubted it, but she had to try, even if it meant watching something stupid. Anything to help her escape the uneasiness.

Eleanor switched the television on. Men wearing tights and chasing after or carrying around a ball invaded the screen. Great! Football. She hated football. If nothing else was on, she might return to it. She changed the channel.

"Damn it," she muttered when Spanish filled the air. She'd forgotten that 21, one of her four channels, was Spanish speaking. A lot of good that did her, although the wildly gesticulating man in his gaudy sequined suit was rather amusing. His scantily clad partner, with long bleach blond hair and big boobs, who bounced up and down next to him added to the feeling of farce emitting from the television. She chuckled and wished she understood at least some of it. Now, this could take her mind off of her own problems.

"Eleanor."

The sound of her name whispered through the house. She clenched her teeth, tamping down the sliver of fear trickling down her spine, clicked to a new channel, and turned up the volume, but the show was *Mysteries of the Unexplained*. The host followed some paranormal psychologists into a haunted house.

"Great," she muttered.

With a press of a button, she changed to the last channel and shuddered. Bloodcurdling screams blared out of the television as a monster chased a young woman through dark, mist-filled woods. Too stupid and too close to her situation. As much as she enjoyed traipsing through the woods during the day, nothing could induce her to brave them at night.

"Eleanor."

Her name came louder this time, piercing through the sound of the television. Her heart raced. A deep, calming breath didn't help. It was just her mind playing tricks on her. If she pretended she didn't hear them, maybe they would go away, whatever "they" were. She flipped it back to the football game, but the game flickered on the screen before returning to *Mysteries of the Unexplained*. Had she pressed the number in error? She tried again, but the scene didn't change. A man with a suitably creepy voice spouted nonsense about ghosts. She dropped the remote control as if it was a live sample of the Ebola virus.

Giggles erupted in the kitchen, and she heard whispering. Goosebumps skittered along her skin. Ruthlessly, she smothered the reaction, grabbed a poker from the fireplace, and crept toward the kitchen. Cold air swirled through the house, and the backdoor slammed with a bang. Just as she suspected it would be, the kitchen was empty. She studied the room, inspecting every inch. Not a trace of another human lurked in the room, but one of the cupboard doors stood open, and a small muddy handprint marked the otherwise clean surface of the back door. When she finally glanced at the window, the imprint of a face stared back at her.

She stifled a scream, even as her legs turned her in the opposite direction and sprinted. In the living room, she stopped, panting as if she'd run a marathon. But it had nothing to do with distance, and she knew it. It was fear.

Damn it. She struggled to control her impulse to flee. She refused to be scared. This house belonged to her. If someone, or some*thing,* else lived here, they would learn to share. Nothing would chase her from her sanctuary.

Maybe she just needed some interpersonal interaction. Maybe it was time she visited her neighbor Lily. Then she laughed at the thought of calling Lily a neighbor. How could you be a neighbor when your houses were five miles apart? She heard another giggle and something that sounded like long nails brushed the side of the house under the living

38

room window.

Eleanor didn't look back. She ran straight to her bedroom and slammed the door, locking it. Another giggle just outside her door cinched her decision. She had to call someone. She needed help. Damn Michael for not leaving his number. Damn her for not asking.

Shaking fingers dialed Officer Tyler's phone number. Five rings later, the sound of his deep voice filtered through the phone line.

"Hello."

"Officer Tyler... I mean, Rodney."

"Yes?"

"It's Eleanor Radcliffe. I'm sorry to be bothering you at home, but I was wondering if you could stop by."

The doorknob jiggled, and something pounded on her bedroom door.

"What was that?" he asked, his tone abrupt.

"I don't know. That's why I called you." She fought to control the panic threatening to overtake her and gripped the poker tighter, but even that didn't inspire confidence. She wanted something more substantial than what now seemed like a thin piece of metal, but other than a bedside lamp, nothing looked promising.

The thing on the other side of the door snarled, and the sound of running feet echoed through the house. A door slammed.

"Stay put. I'll be right there."

The line went dead.

Because going outside would be a good idea?

She hung up and tried to still the shudders rippling through her body. If she could just hang on until Rodney arrived, she'd be fine. Better yet, if she only had some way to contact Michael...

Chapter Seven

The longest ten minutes of her life passed before car lights flashed through her bedroom window and the sound of gravel crunching under tires filtered through the night air. On shaking legs, Eleanor stood. Was it safe to leave the bedroom? Did she have a choice?

She paused with her hand on the doorknob. Still locked, she hesitated to open it.

"Eleanor? Are you there?" Loud knocking accompanied the question.

The sound of Rodney's voice gave her courage to unlock her bedroom door and venture out into the living room. She ran to the front door and threw it open. Her arms reached for him, but he grabbed her shoulders then gently pried the poker from her grasp.

"Are you okay?" Concern filled his voice and broke the dam that had held her tears at bay.

She collapsed against him, sobbing.

He gathered her in his arms and shushed her. "It's okay. I'm here." He maneuvered them back into the room, shut the door behind them, and sat her down on the couch. "Can you tell me what happened?"

She nodded and huddled against his warm bulk. With a deep breath, she struggled to control the tears slipping down her cheeks and finally managed to stop crying after a few minutes. The words tumbled out of her, punctuated with sniffles and the occasional hiccup.

"This is the worst I've ever heard of it being."

She stared at him hard. "What do you mean?"

His hesitation told her more than she wanted to know. He hadn't been straight with her.

"You don't think it's neighborhood kids either, do you?" The words came out accusing.

"I..." A flush crept up his neck, proclaiming his guilt. "There's no other explanation," he said and rushed on. "What else could it be?"

"I don't know, but I can tell you that whatever ran its fingernails down the side of my house was *not* a child. And if it was, their nails have to be harder than a horse's hooves."

"Do you have someone you can stay with? If not, you are welcome to stay in my spare room for a few days." Warmth filled his deep brown eyes. "I promise you, nothing would happen."

Eleanor opened her mouth, not sure how she wanted to respond, but the shrill ringing of the phone saved her from any embarrassing gibberish bound to come out of her mouth.

"Do you want me to get that?" he asked.

"No." As if poked with a red-hot branding iron, she leapt off the couch and raced into the kitchen. She kept her gaze focused on the phone, refusing to look at, or out of, any of the windows.

"Hello," she answered. The heavy weight of hands settled on her shoulders, startling her. She looked up, her gaze meeting Rodney's, and he squeezed her shoulders. A tight smile drew her face taut. She couldn't manage more than that.

"Eleanor?" Lily's blithe voice sparkled through the phone line.

Eleanor smiled despite herself. "Yes?"

"Are you alone?"

"Um..."

"Oh, I'm sorry. I hope I'm not interrupting anything..."

"No. No, you aren't." Eleanor rushed to assure her. "What's up?"

"Well, now I'm not sure if I should ask, but, you know, you can't know unless you ask. Matter of fact, if you never ask, you'll never know now, will you?" Lily laughed a little. "Anyway, my kids have gone to visit their grandmother for a few days. You know, I didn't realize how lonely I would be without them here. The fog has been particularly dense around our house, and my husband has a couple of farmer's meetings he has to attend the next couple of nights, so I am going to be all alone."

Eleanor could almost see Lily shudder and smiled.

"I thought a couple of days with no one but myself to please would be simply divine. Hah! I need chaos, or at

41

the very least, another warm body in the house. Even my husband, sweet man that he is, isn't enough, especially when he won't be home for another hour or so. I know it's late, but do you think you could come for a visit just for a few days? I've been thinking about and been wondering how you are getting along. Maybe we could have some nice, long chats... provided I let you speak at all. You're so quiet." Her chuckle filled the air. "Do you have siblings? I can't imagine anyone who has siblings being so quiet. Why my children... Well, there I go again. I can't seem to shut up long enough for you to answer me." She paused. "So, will you? I'd love to have a woman to chat with for the next couple of days... That is if you don't have any other plans."

"I..." Eleanor's gaze met Rodney's. She liked him. He was a nice, strong man, but staying at his house so soon, even if it was well intentioned? She couldn't do it. Now, if it had been Michael... No. Michael wasn't here and wasn't likely to come as she had no way to contact him and didn't know if she would if she could. The intensity of her feelings for him scared her. "I don't have any other plans. And thank you. I'd be delighted."

"Wonderful," Lily exclaimed.

Eleanor envisioned Lily clapping her hands in delight and smiled again. "Great. I'll gather my stuff then."

"You are a peach to be so amenable. I'll see you soon then."

Eleanor hung up with a smile and trepidation. What to say to Rodney?

"Rodney..." She looked at him and decided that honesty was the best choice. "I like you, but I don't know you well enough to stay at your house regardless of how innocent it might be." She paused, trying to gauge his reaction. His expression gave nothing away, so she rushed on before her courage disappeared. "I still want to see you, but my neighbor Lily just asked me to visit, and I think it might be best if I stayed with her instead." She searched his face for some sign of emotion.

His expression remained impassive before a smile slowly relaxed it, lighting up his handsome features. He nodded. "It's okay. You're being smart. I like smart women."

Warmth filled her at his comment, and the tension began to uncoil a little at a time. "Good. Because I like you, too." She couldn't contain a smile. She didn't want to.

"Do you mind if I stick around and drive you over to her house?" he asked.

He wanted her safe. His concern made her feel special. "I'd like that." She lightly touched his arm. "Thank you."

"My pleasure."

She turned toward her bedroom and stopped. "I know this is going to sound silly, but could you come with me to the bedroom? Even though it's been quiet for a bit, I'm still a little spooked."

He took her hand and smiled down at her. "No problem."

They walked first to her bedroom where she packed a small bag then to her bathroom for her toiletries. As they left each room, they turned the lights off. She took her jacket and hat out of the front closet and grabbed her keys. With one last look around her living room, she flicked the porch light on, opened the front door, and turned off the last light in the house. She stepped closer to Rodney, gripping his hand, and shut the door behind her. The click of the lock echoed loudly through the fog-laden night air.

Rodney ushered her to the car and held the door for her. Hurrying around the front of the car, he jumped in next to her, started the car, and drove away. Eleanor glanced back and watched the fog slowly consume her house. On the periphery of the porch light's penetration into the fog, child-sized figures seemed to hover. The porch light flickered, making the figures appear to dance. For a moment, she thought she heard high keening wails, and the fine hair at the back of her neck stood on end. Goosebumps raced across her skin, and she shuddered. She jerked around and looked at Rodney. Had he heard it? But he remained silent. His gaze fixed on the road ahead. She shivered and hunkered down in her seat.

Chapter Eight

No sooner did Rodney pull the car out of her driveway than the fog wrapped around them like a white cocoon. Eleanor strained to see the road ahead of them, grateful Rodney was driving and not her. The headlights revealed one yellow-dashed line at a time. Rodney slowed the car to a crawl. Unable to help herself, she searched the side of the road for any sign of the figures she'd seen just moments before in front of her house. Not a religious person, she mentally prayed she wouldn't.

"It's only a few miles up the road on the right side, but at this pace, it might take us a while to reach Lily's house." Rodney's deep voice broke the silence.

"It wasn't this bad when you drove to my house, was it?" Guilt plagued her at the thought of him driving in this to come and help her.

"No. It must have rolled in during the short time I was at your house."

She breathed a sigh of relief. "Good."

All of a sudden, the fog lifted enough to see to the next patch of fog. Silver pillows of mist rested low to the ground like airy blankets. Overhead, stars studded the sky, their frozen brilliance stark against the ink black sky. A small cloud resembling a gauze scarf drifted across the road. It swirled around their car as they passed through it.

"Ghost dust," Rodney said, chuckling.

Eleanor looked at him, and all the hair on her body stood on end. She shook it off. "Ghost dust?"

"Some of the locals refer to that type of drifting fog as 'ghost dust.'"

She didn't respond and watched the hills slip by. After the events of this night, the possibility of it being something not human at her house was very likely. Even joking about ghosts in any form sent a quiver of anxiety shooting through her.

"Do you know where Lily lives?"

"Lily Johanson?"

Eleanor smiled. "As you know her last name, I imagine you do then."

"Yes, of course. Her family has been out here for years. Or I should say that the Johanson spread has been here for years. Most of the farms have passed down from one generation to the next. They're nice people. How did you meet her?" he inquired.

"She stopped by and introduced herself." A chuckle escaped her at the thought of their first meeting. "Lily's a, um, character."

The deep rumble of his chuckle joined hers. "Yes, she is, but she's a good woman to know."

He slowed the car and turned off onto a paved driveway. A white wooden arch straddled the road. Johanson Ranch followed by a circled J filled the top of the arch. The path wound up and around the rolling hills. At the crest of the third hill, they looked down into a small depression. Dense fog had settled into it. A tiny ray of light pierced through the encroaching mist, affirming a house stood somewhere in it.

"Almost there," he said.

With that, they descended into the fog. A few minutes later, the car rolled to a stop in front of a two story white house. The lower quarter of the house was made from river rock. On top of the stone, a large veranda with a waist-high railing and rectangular pillars at regular intervals wrapped around the front of the house. Three stone steps led up to the front door. A cushioned chair sat next to a porch swing. A table separated the chair from the swing.

Eleanor had always wanted a house like this. She could envision herself sitting on the porch swing on a balmy summer evening, enjoying the quiet of the countryside and watching for falling stars. Crickets would chirp, frogs would ribbit, and owls would hoot, creating a symphony not found in the city.

The door swung open. Light outlined Lily's tall, slender body. Even with the porch light on, Lily's face was in shadows, but Eleanor imagined there was a smile on it. Eleanor grinned in return. The next couple of days promised to be interesting.

Eleanor opened her door, grabbed her purse and overnight case, and followed Rodney up the front steps.

"It took you long enough," Lily said. "I was beginning to wonder if you had decided to walk, although I wouldn't recommend doing that in this weather. Our roads may not be that busy, but we do have the occasional yahoo who thinks it's their very own race track." She rolled her eyes and ushered them in the house, closing the door firmly behind them. "Kids can be utterly stupid." She took their coats and hung them up on the pegs next to the door. "If you don't mind leaving your shoes next to the door, that would be great. We just installed new carpets throughout the house. Well, where there aren't hardwood floors, of course."

Lily turned and started up the stairs that lay cattycorner from the front door on the left side of the foyer. Next to the stairs, a hall led to the back of the house. An entry table cluttered with keys, paper, and bric-a-brac crowded the hallway under the stairs.

In stocking-covered feet, Lily moved upward past walls covered with family photos and paintings, most obviously created by young children. "I'll show you to your room first, if you don't mind, so you can put your things away. Unfortunately, you'll have to share the kid's bathroom. Fortunately, it's just been cleaned, and they aren't here. With all four of them at home, that bathroom is a disaster area."

She smiled over her shoulder and continued up without waiting for them. At the top of the stairs, she turned right. A few steps on, and she disappeared into the upper regions of the house. Her voice still carried, but the words were muffled.

Bemused, Eleanor's gaze met Rodney's. A smile lurked in his eyes. With a shake of her head, she knelt down, removed her shoes, and set them neatly next to the row of shoes lined up under the hanging coats. Retrieving her purse and overnight case, she started to follow Lily up the stairs.

On the first step, she turned back to Rodney. "I'm okay now if you want to go home."

"Are you trying to get rid of me?" A smile took the bite out of the question.

"No, but it's late, the fog is dense, and it will probably only grow worse as the night wears on." She returned to his

Marci Baun

side and placed a hand on his arm. "Look, I really appreciate what you did for me tonight. I can't tell you how much it meant to me."

"I'm glad I could help you."

"Well, I can't thank you enough."

He grinned. "But you could go out with me."

"Yes, I could." Bubbles of pleasure tickled her insides, prompting an answering grin.

"I'll be off again in a week's time. How about a date?"

"Call me."

"I will." He leaned down and chastely kissed her lips.

Desire pooled inside of her. It wasn't a raging inferno, but a quiet, comfortable kind of "I want", completely unlike the ravenous beast Michael's elicited. She delicately licked her lips, savoring his unique flavor. His eyes darkened with desire. She leaned in for another taste.

"Eleanor?"

At the sound of Lily's voice, Rodney smiled crookedly at her. "I'll call you soon," he said and slipped out of the door.

Chapter Nine

"Are you sure I didn't interrupt anything tonight? You could have said 'no'," Lily said as she descended the staircase.

"Positive," Eleanor replied.

"Are you sure? That Officer Tyler is one hunky man." Lily winked at her.

"We just met, so I'm taking it slow. I like him, but..."

"I understand completely. 'Why buy the cow when you can have the milk for free,' my mother always used to say. She was right. You have to make a man earn it. Whatever 'it' might be." Lily started up the stairs again. "Besides," she said, grinning over her shoulder, "it's fun to make them sweat. Nothing like a man raring to go, you know." She winked at her.

Eleanor shook her head and laughed, glad she'd come to stay with Lily. Her nonsensical, upbeat chatter was exactly what she needed to shake the quivering fear that still gripped her in its iron fist.

"How long have you and your husband been married?" she asked.

"Longer than a dinosaur's fart is old." Lily laughed and turned right at the top of the stairs. "Okay, maybe not that long, but sometimes it feels like it." She stopped so quickly Eleanor nearly ran her over. Her face soft with love, Lily's smile spoke of true love, happiness, and a contentment most people rarely found. "We met in college, so that would be... fifteen years? Urgh! I'm getting old."

She waved her hand as if that would sweep away the melancholy. "Can you imagine," her gaze connected with Eleanor's, "I met him in physics class?" A soft laugh danced around the room. "Me? In physics?" The laugh grew louder. "I tutored him, you know. Ditzy Lily." Her eyes twinkled. "Yes, I know how airheadish I appear. Don't let that fool you." She grinned and winked. "It's all a front."

Eleanor chuckled. "I never thought you were stupid. Eccentric. Quirky. Funny. Stupid? No."

"See, you're smart, too. No wonder I like you." Lily opened a door at the end of the hall and entered. "You'll be staying in my eldest daughter's room. She's the cleanest of the bunch. When we built this house, we'd intended on having one guest room, but," she shrugged, "we had one more child than expected." She grinned. "It happens that way sometimes. Anyway, don't worry about Jess minding about her room. The kids are always displaced when visitors come to stay. And with Jess visiting her grandmother, it doesn't matter. Besides, I'm sure she'll like you when she meets you. Well, she likes almost everyone." Laughter flashed in her blue eyes. "I don't know where she got *that* trait."

A smile quirked Eleanor's lips. If the daughter was anything like her mother, she'd be delightful. And, judging from the room's décor, she imagined Jess took after her mother quite a bit, although unlike her mother, Jess didn't seem to have the need to fill her room with "dust collectors."

Not frilly, but definitely girlish, three large daisy flowers in hot pink, lime green, and purple with white centers contrasted with the pale aqua walls. A white vanity sat next to the closet door. Simple, white curtains tied back with hot pink skull-dotted sashes framed the large window that looked out onto the front yard. Four furry pillows, hot pink, lime green, purple, and pale aqua, popped against the white bedspread. A lamp with a purple shade with white peace signs graced the white bedside table. Aqua fringe rimmed the bottom of the shade. Under the lamp rested a book. Not one article of clothing marred the lime green carpet. It was a fun room—seventies revisited with a modern twist.

"No posters?" Eleanor asked, remembering her own room when she was a teenager. She had at least one teen idol up on the wall.

Lily shrugged. "Jess says she doesn't want her room cluttered with posters." She grinned. "However, she put one up where she could see it all of the time, since she practically lives with her door closed."

Swinging the door shut, she moved out of the way. A teen idol smiled back at them. Eleanor recognized him, but didn't remember his name.

"I look forward to meeting her," Eleanor said.

"Yes, well, not for a few days at least. Now that I have you here, I don't want to share you with my brood yet. They'd be all over you. You think I talk a lot?" She laughed. "Nothing compared to my children. Your ears will ring for days after one session with them. My ears have long since grown used to the cacophony, but I fear you'll need to be introduced to them gently, or they might drive you insane." She grinned. "All right. I'm going downstairs to make us some...what would you like: Coffee? Tea? Hot chocolate?"

"Coffee sounds wonderful."

"All right, then, you come down when you're ready. I'll be there."

She shut the door, and the room descended into silence. Eleanor walked over to the window and looked out. Fog covered the land, a silver blanket with the icy stars shining above as if nothing odd had happened that night.

Turning from the window, Eleanor moved her bag next to the vanity. She looked around the room again and went in search of the bathroom.

She walked a short distance down the hall to the kid's bathroom and stepped in. Kid friendly and incredibly clean, white tile sparkled at her. Dark blue towels hung on chrome towel racks. Cheery fish soap sat in the soap dish next to each of the two basins. A mirror lined the wall above the basins. The toilet was on the right hand side of the room across from the basins. Along the back wall, a tiled bathtub rested next to a shower with glass doors.

Eager to join Lily, Eleanor quickly finished her business and stepped out into the hall. The sound of voices startled her. Lily had said her husband would be home late, and Rodney had already left. Curious, she moved toward the landing and jerked back at the sight that greeted her. Down below, Michael and Lily spoke softly. Occasionally, her name drifted up toward her. Lily gestured up toward the bedrooms, obviously annoyed with Michael. Her voice grew louder with each gesture until Eleanor could hear them clearly.

"I disagree, Michael. We have to tell her. She'll be safer if we do."

"We can't, Lily. You know the rules. It puts her at greater risk if she knows."

"Do you have any idea what kind of risk she's in now? I heard them keening tonight, Michael. *Keening.* I haven't heard that in decades. You know what happened the last time they did that. They want her, and if we don't do something soon, they'll get her."

Angry and frightened, Eleanor stepped out from her hiding place, determined to find out what was going on, and asked, "Who wants me?"

Chapter Ten

Michael's startled gaze met hers. "Uh..."

"We have to tell her, Michael," Lily said.

"The more she knows..."

"You said that already."

"It's against—"

"The rules only apply in normal circumstances. Hers have long passed the normal circumstances, and it's only been a few weeks." She turned to Eleanor. For once, her eyes didn't sparkle with mirth. "You are in serious danger. The—"

"Lily—"

"No. She is. It's true."

"Do you want to bring them to your house?" Michael asked.

"They've already tried. Their excitement is palpable. I can feel it pulling on the strands that hold the doorways closed. Why do you think I knew to call tonight? We can't delay any longer. Something must be done."

Lily crossed to the window, pulled back the drapes, and motioned to the world outside. Eleanor couldn't help herself. She stared out the window. Condensation clung to the glass. Lily's porch light barely penetrated the fog that seethed and writhed as if trying to hold back something.

"Even now, they try to breach our defenses. In the past, they've stuck to tormenting whoever lives there to drive them off. You know as well as I that as soon as I bring the person here, they settle back to wait. For some reason, they want her."

Lily's blue gaze bored into her, taking in her hair and figure, all trace of the scatterbrained blonde gone. "But why?" Her shrewd gaze moved back to Michael, who looked away.

"I have my suspicions," he said.

She narrowed her eyes at Eleanor. "Is she?"

He nodded. "But that doesn't always—"

"Am I what?" Eleanor asked, clenching her hands.

Michael's gaze shuttered when he looked at her. "It's something we can't discuss with you."

"She needs to know."

"What do I need to know?" Eleanor turned to Lily, who averted her gaze, and then Michael, whose mouth tightened in a hard line.

"We can't, Lily. Not yet."

"Then when? How much more dire does it need to get?" Lily asked.

"Not yet," Michael said and crossed his arms, his face an unreadable mask.

"All right, is there anything else we should know? Anything else that could've caused this reaction?" Lily nibbled at her lip and stared at her house guest.

Images of her vivid dream two night's past bombarded Eleanor's mind, and heat suffused her face. Unable to meet the other woman's scrutiny, she turned her attention to the stairs and descended them. When she reached the bottom, she took a deep breath and walked over to the window.

"Michael, what did you do?"

"Nothing. We did nothing."

Some emotion flickered across his face too fast for Eleanor to decipher. She spun around. *So it had been a dream?* Relief washed over her. Sex after the second day of knowing someone was too soon. But it had been so real.

"Then why did she blush?"

"We kissed," Eleanor blurted out, hoping her blush didn't reveal that she'd wanted much more.

"You kissed? Well, that changes nothing." She cocked her head and chuckled. "You kissed her, Michael? I'm surprised." She looked at Eleanor and smiled. "Not that you aren't attractive, just that he's never done that before. Rodney was quite taken with you, too. There must be something about you that appeals to men. I'm not insulting you, mind you. You have beautiful hair and beautiful eyes and a nice figure. There's a sparkle about you, too, that I didn't notice before."

Eleanor squirmed under Lily's inspection, and, for the second time that evening, she blushed. For heaven's sake, she wasn't a schoolgirl. She was an adult. If she wanted to fantasize about a hot cowboy who happened to be a neighbor, she could. It wasn't anyone's business but her own.

"We, um..." Michael cleared his throat. His intense gaze pinned Eleanor to her spot, and more heat rushed to her cheeks.

This was becoming ridiculous. Michael had only kissed her. It had been just a kiss, and then he'd disappeared. No number. Nothing. It wasn't like he could read her mind or knew about her dream.

A chuckle erupted from Lily. "Finally, someone's broken through your icy exterior. Michael's smitten. It's good to see you fall for someone, but that doesn't explain their interest in her. Not even sex would. It's a good thing the brood isn't home. We're going to have to take her some place safer. She can't stay here." Lily moved down a hallway off to the left and deeper into the house, still talking. Her voice echoed behind her, and she turned a corner. "I'll contact Joseph and Angela and let them know we are coming—"

Eleanor turned to Michael, fear, anger, and confusion warring inside of her. "What does she mean, *I'm not safe here?* Who're Joseph and Angela? And what the hell is going on? And what am I?"

Something hit the window behind her with a loud thud. She spun and screamed, bumping into Michael as she backed away from the creature staring back at her, its childlike face frightening. Ashen skin drawn tight across the sharp angles of its bones, the thing snarled, and pointed teeth glistened when it smiled. Tangled, black hair hung past its shoulders. Eyes devoid of all color and no whites stared back at her. A long, snake-like tongue flicked out, licking its thin lips.

"Eleanor..."

The sibilant whisper slipped up her spine, and she shivered.

"Come to me, Eleanor."

All of her instincts told her to run, but her body refused to listen, and she stepped toward the door.

"No!" Strong arms wrapped around her, and, suddenly, she was looking into Michael's tawny eyes. "Eleanor, can you hear me?"

Eye contact broken with the creature, she regained control of her body. Terrified and unable to speak, she nodded. Behind her, the creature keened. The sound of nails on glass set her body to trembling. She started to look over her shoulder, but Michael grabbed her face.

"No. Do not look at it."

Lily rushed into the room, her blond hair flying around her. "What the hell is—" She slid to a halt and grabbed Eleanor's arm, pulling her down the hall. "Oh, my God. We must leave *now*. Do you understand, Eleanor?"

Again, Eleanor could only nod. Her mind struggled to process what she'd seen. The trembling increased until her teeth chattered. Her movements slowed, and darkness swallowed her sight until only a pinprick of light remained. Then the light completely disappeared, and she was falling into an abyss.

* * * *

"Well, that explains why the Gehglers want her."

Lily's voice filtered into Eleanor's consciousness as if from a great distance. Her head throbbed, and her body ached as if she'd fallen off a cliff. Groggy, she lay still, shifting in and out of the darkness hovering at the edge of her mind and listening.

"Thank God you grabbed her arm when she started to collapse. They might have found her before we did."

The sound of footsteps drawing closer echoed in a... room? As her mind woke more fully, more details sifted through the dream gauze that was slowly releasing its grasp on her. Someone had laid her on something soft. A bed? Why was she lying down? The last thing she remembered...

Surely, it had been a dream. That thing she'd seen in the window had to have been a dream. She'd find herself at Lily's house in her daughter's room. It would be morning, and fog would still blanket the countryside.

Eager to prove herself right, she opened her eyes. Solid wooden beams greeted her instead of the white drywall ceiling she was expecting. Panic galvanized her, and she sat up.

"What the—"

"Oh, good, you're awake," Lily said and crossed the room.

Large windows looked out into a foreign landscape. Plants she didn't recognize, but that obviously belonged in a desert, grew out of rich, red soil. A soil so red could only be in one place: Sedona, Arizona. How did she...

Her heart raced. The world spun. She swayed. A rush of heat coursed through her veins, and she fought the nausea that rose in her throat. Chaotic thoughts trampled each other, each fighting for dominance in her mind. Could she have been so wrong about Michael and Lily? Were they really human traffickers? Were those creatures and all the odd happenings just a ploy to get her to trust them and make it easy for them to kidnap her?

"Eleanor?"

The concern in Michael's voice snapped her out of her wild thoughts. Surely, there was a logical explanation for everything.

She turned to face him and swung her legs over the bed. Again, the room whirled around her. She gripped the edge of the bed and breathed deeply to stop the spinning. His warm hands steadied her, and she looked up, grateful for his support, yet still leery of him. A sense of safety and peace swept through her as his golden gaze caught hers. He'd never harm her. Somehow, she knew this. She smiled.

A smile lit his eyes first and spread across his entire face to his lips. Kindness mixed with interest reached across the short distance and warmed her. How could she have ever doubted him?

"Are you two done?" Lily asked, laughing.

Eleanor blushed, averting her eyes from his, trying to focus on anything but the attraction blazing between them. But it was hard. His very essence drew her. Even the brown, flannel shirt, something that would normally not turn her on, sent her pulse racing. Snug blue jeans hugged his hips. And his hands...

She looked down at her hands and then up at Michael and Lily. She had to get a grip on herself. If those things were real, she was in danger. If they weren't and her two "friends" were human traffickers, she was in danger. Neither option appealed to her.

"What's going on? Where am I? And how did I—we—get

here?"

A guarded expression flashed across Lily's face. "Well..." Her gaze darted from Michael to Eleanor and back to Michael. He nodded. "I..."

"This isn't something we're supposed to discuss with others. I'm not even sure we should be telling you, but," Michael glanced at Lily, "considering what happened last night—"

"Michael—"

"I agree with you, Lily, we have no choice," Michael said. "We not only heard them, but saw them. When was the last time that happened?"

A taut silence stretched between them. Minutes ticked by as the two seemed to grapple with the situation. Eleanor said nothing and waited, unsure whether she wanted to know the truth or not and certain she wasn't prepared for it.

Before they could say anything, a woman entered the room and smiled at Eleanor. Black, curly hair cascaded over her shoulders, and fine lines traced the corners of her warm, brown eyes. "It's good to see you're finally awake. The first time using the ley lines can be very tiring."

Eleanor stared at her in confusion.

"Oh, I see." The woman looked at Michael and Lily. "You haven't explained what happened yet?"

"Well..." Michael started.

The woman nodded. "Well, we'll rectify that now."

"Are you sure, Angela?" Lily asked.

"Yes," Angela said. "Come, I suggest we discuss this over breakfast." She walked to the door and looked back over her shoulder. "You'll feel much better after eating."

Eleanor's stomach grumbled, and, suddenly, she realized she was ravenous.

Chapter Eleven

"Here." Angela set a plate of pancakes in front of her on a round table. "You can eat while we talk."

Eleanor nodded. The aroma of butter, maple syrup, and pancakes tickled her nose, and her stomach grumbled again. She took a bite, and the pancake nearly melted on her tongue. She closed her eyes, forgetting everything but the divine flavors assaulting her senses. "Mm..."

Michael's laughter filled the room. Her eyes popped open.

"What?"

He grinned. "Everyone reacts that way the first time they taste Angela's pancakes. She's the mistress of pancakes."

Angela smacked his arm. "Oh, really, Michael. They're just pancakes."

"These are not 'just pancakes.' These are far beyond that." She took another bite, her eyes closing in pleasure again. Each bite was like a mini orgasm in her mouth. She blushed at the thought of the comparison, but it was the truth.

"Do you think you can focus so we can talk?"

Michael's amused voice broke into her haze of pleasure. His question sobered her, and memories of the night before crowded in on her. Fear skittered along her nerve endings as images of the creature filled her mind. She shook her head to dispel the terrifying visual. Taking a deep breath, she nodded.

"Perhaps we should start with what's been happening," Angela suggested. "It might be best if you told us everything."

"I..."

Eleanor studied their faces. All of them regarded her with a seriousness that scared her. She glanced down at her hands gripping the utensils, her knuckles white. She gently placed them on the table and stared blindly at the remaining pancakes. How much should she tell them? Would they think her crazy if she did? Somehow, she doubted they would.

Still, she didn't know if she wanted to join their world. Once the conversation began, her life would change forever. Solid, black eyes flitted across her mind's eye. Her life had changed already. She couldn't go home and pretend nothing was there. That thing wanted her. If it got her...she shuddered. That thing, and its ilk, had chased her from her home, her haven, where she had gone to heal and find some peace. Now, she had nothing.

Anger slowly overtook the fear. It grew, and she knew what she had to do. Starting with the appearance of the path, all the way to what had happened the night before, she told them everything. Still unwilling to meet their gazes, she stared at her hands in her lap.

A deep silence fell when she stopped. A clock ticked somewhere in the house. The silence stretched, but she couldn't bring herself to see their expressions. What if she judged them wrong? What if they thought she was crazy? Despite her resolve, fear of seeing their reaction paralyzed her. Only when Michael reached over and caressed her hand did she look up.

Concern had etched itself on their faces.

"We had no idea it had escalated to that level until last night," Lily said. "Had we known, I would've invited you over sooner."

"This behavior hasn't happened since you became a keeper, Lily," Angela said.

"I didn't think it was this bad." Lily stood up and walked to the window. "We heard them keening."

"Keening..."

The tone of Angela's voice sent a shiver down Eleanor's spine.

"Did you leave anything out?" Angela asked.

Eleanor glanced at Michael. Heat rose in her cheeks. "No."

Angela's eyes narrowed. She looked between Michael and Eleanor. "Are you sure?"

"I...I had a dream, but I don't think that matters. It was a dream, after all." Eleanor sneaked a peek at Michael again. A deep flush spread across his cheeks, and a chill ran down her spine. The memory of the hair floating in the tub surfaced.

It was a dream, right? Just a fantasy. It had to be a fantasy. That couldn't have happened. Could it?

"Michael, what did you do?" Lily stared at him accusingly.

"I didn't *do* anything. I heard her call my name, and then, suddenly, I was there at her house."

Eleanor's stomach dropped. "What?" Her voice came out in a squeak.

"You didn't initiate the travel?" Angela's voice cut through the silence.

"No," Michael said. He stood and joined Lily at the window. Turning back toward the table, he leaned against the sill and crossed his arms. Frustration and guilt emanated from him.

"What are you saying?" Eleanor asked.

The Lily Eleanor knew had completely disappeared. Her blue eyes stared back at her, a mixture of awe and concern in them. "You summoned Michael with a dream, Eleanor," she said. "And you didn't think that information was important, Michael?"

"Well—"

"No, I didn't *summon* anyone. It *was* a dream, just a dream. Wasn't it?" She turned to Michael. "Wasn't it?"

He looked away.

It had been real. They had made love. Her stomach dropped, and the pancakes that had tasted like manna a few moments before settled like a stone in her stomach. Bile rose in her throat.

A kaleidoscope of emotions rushed through her, horror, shame, excitement. For the first time in her life, the woman who never did anything that she shouldn't—not including selling her parents' house and moving to Fresno against her family's advice—had done the unthinkable and had sex with a strange man. Granted, she'd thought she was dreaming. What would her old-fashioned parents think if they were alive still?

But they weren't alive. With her relatives so far away, no one would know. No one would tell them. No one who knew her was there to see her blush and stammer if she tried to lie. For all intents and purposes, she was alone. A whole new world opened up to her.

It was frightening and...liberating.

"Eleanor, are you okay?"

Lily's voice pierced her thoughts, and she nodded. "Yes. Yes. At least, I think am." Fear bubbled beneath her new determination to change and live her life her way. She had to understand this new life that appeared to be taking over hers. "What do you mean by 'summon?' And what are ley lines?"

"The earth is covered in a grid of energy. These lines are called ley lines. They crisscross and encircle the earth and have been used for centuries by ancient societies and advanced races. But the use of these lines comes with a price, especially when misused or overused." Angela paused, took a sip of her tea, and set her mug down on the table. "Overuse, and misuse, opens the veil between parallel universes. Some of these universes are home to creatures like the Gehglers. Others have humanoids like us, with varying degrees of psychic abilities and technological advances. And there are others with creatures that make Gehglers look as friendly as puppies. Fortunately, the denizens of those worlds have no interest in ours."

Hysterical laughter lodged in Eleanor's throat. Parallel universes, scary creatures, ley lines, all of these belonged in science fiction/fantasy books. They didn't exist in the real world. Black eyes devoid of any other color flashed in her mind's eye. *It wasn't real. I dreamed it.*

She looked over to the window. Outside, the red rock of Sedona mocked her. As illogical as all of this sounded, she couldn't deny her experiences.

Her legs threatened to collapse at the realization that everything they told her could be true. She gripped the windowsill, the world spinning. Warm hands grabbed her arms and guided her to a chair. Her legs gave way, and she sat, staring stupidly in front of her.

"It is a bit much to take in," Lily said, "especially if you haven't lived with the knowledge that some day you might become a keeper."

For a few minutes, she breathed deeply. Fear ripped at her sanity. It couldn't win. Not if she wanted to survive. She had to accept her new reality, now, if she intended on seeing tomorrow. Panic attacks wouldn't help her. Her gut told her she didn't have the luxury of one.

Although fear swirled on the edge of her consciousness, it no longer impeded her ability to think.

"So, what do I do now?" Eleanor asked. "And how do I avoid the Gehglers?"

"Avoiding the Gehglers will work only for so long. Any ley line you can use, they can, too. And they want you, so they will find you. While we can protect you, there will come a day when you must be able to protect yourself. It is our job to teach you those skills." Angela stood and put her empty cup in the sink. She returned to her seat at the table and continued. "The ley lines here are protected by many people. Some are keepers. You should be safe...for now, but," she glanced at the other two, "I'm concerned. Summoning takes great skill and energy. Opening a ley line and traveling one also requires training and practice. You have done both without conscious thought. We must start training you for your protection and ours."

Anxious to get her life back under control, Eleanor leaned forward and asked, "How do we begin?"

Over the next few hours, the four of them planned their next moves. Eleanor would stay with Angela for at least a week, if not two. Her training would begin after lunch. Lily had to return home, but she would be flying out tomorrow to avoid the use of ley lines. Her kids would be returning from their grandparents' house tomorrow evening. She needed to be there when they arrived. She'd keep in touch by phone and report any unusual activities. Michael would remain for a couple more days.

At the end of the session, Angela rose. "Why don't we take a break? This has been pretty intense. We can meet back here in an hour for lunch."

Grateful, Eleanor stood. Her mind spinning from all of the information they'd discussed, she relished a bit of solitude.

Chapter Twelve

"Why don't you go sit on the patio by the fountain?" Angela suggested. "I always find that to be soothing. It helps to clear my mind."

Eleanor nodded. "That would be lovely."

"You'll want a jacket. Just borrow one from the front closet. Michael can show you where it is, if you don't mind. I'll just finish cleaning up here and start lunch."

"Oh, no. Let me help."

Angela waved her away. "You need some down time before we start our training. I find the sounds of nature are amazing at clearing one's mind." She reached for a cup and poured some hot tea. Handing it to Eleanor, she said, "This will help keep your hands and insides warm out there."

Eleanor took the tea and smiled, the heat already transferring to her hands. "Thank you."

"Do you mind if I come with you?" Michael asked. "A bit of peace and quiet sounds good to me, too."

Eleanor suspected he didn't want to leave her alone, even if it was supposed to be safe here. Part of her appreciated his desire to protect her. Another part resented it. At this moment, she craved solitude.

"Sure."

"Follow me," he said.

He turned and walked down the hall. They stopped by the front closet where she picked out a heavy fleece before he led her outside to the patio.

Large oak trees towered over a sitting area. In the hotter months, their leaves would protect the area from the brutal strength of the sun. At that moment, their bare limbs stretched toward an impossibly blue sky. Eleanor sat on one of the black wrought iron chairs that surrounded a large matching table and took a sip of her tea. Setting the cup down, she rubbed her arms. Angela had been right. Despite the blue sky, the crisp air nipped at her even through the fleece jacket.

"It's beautiful here," she said. "If it weren't for the red rock and soil and sagebrush—oh, and no fog and brown grass—I could almost imagine myself back in Fresno with all of these oaks. I thought Sedona was a desert."

"It is. Angela lives near Oak Creek. The further away you go from the creek, the more you'll see the conifers, sagebrush, and cacti. While I visit Angela on occasion, I'm not an expert on this area. She can tell you more if you want to know. My knowledge strictly lies with my home turf." He smiled.

"Regardless, I can see the appeal of living here."

Eleanor picked up her cup and sipped at the tea. The liquid trickled down her throat and warmed her insides. She closed her eyes and enjoyed the quiet. Some little animal scampered in the dry leaves that carpeted the ground. A hawk cried in the distance, and birds twittered in the trees. Her fear retreated to a faint echo, dissipating as the sounds of nature soothed her shattered nerves. She sighed and allowed herself to relax.

"It's been a wild couple of days for you."

She opened her eyes. "Yes, it has."

Taking another sip, she studied him over the rim of her cup. He stared off into the brush, a thoughtful look on his face. His strong jaw, soft lips, thick brown hair, and the slight bump that prevented his nose from being straight in profile set her stomach to fluttering. The memory of their interlude in the bathtub swirled in her mind. Desire curled in her belly, intensifying with each moment. She wanted him.

He turned to her, and their gazes collided. Heat rushed to her face. She tried to look away, but she was captivated. His golden eyes turned molten. He reached for her. She leaned in and closed her eyes. Warm liquid splashed on her shirt.

"Darn it," she said. "I hope the tea doesn't stain Angela's fleece." She stood, patting at the tea spots and spilling more of the tea.

He stood, took the cup from her hands, and set it on the table. "Forget about the tea."

Cupping her face, he brushed butterfly kisses across her forehead to the tip of her nose. When he came to her lips, he paused and gazed into her eyes as if asking permission.

Passion had turned his face into all angles and planes.

Marci Baun

Never had she seen any man as sexy as Michael. The desire that had curled in her belly a few minutes earlier exploded into a raging inferno and streaked through her. She reached for him. She wanted his body pressed against hers, needed him inside of her.

"More," she demanded and wrapped her arms around his neck, pulling his head down.

"I've been wanting to do this all morning."

The rumble of his voice danced along her nerve endings. She gasped at the sensations coursing through her right before their lips met with the ferocity of long denied passion. His tongue skimmed the surface of her lips, and she opened for him. He slid his fingers into her hair, holding her head in place. Moaning, she glided her hands down his back and grabbed his butt, grinding her hips against his.

He groaned and broke the kiss. His breathing ragged, he cuddled her against his chest and said, "We must stop before I can't." He placed a kiss on top of her head and then rested his on top of hers. "This is not the place for what I want to do to you."

She struggled to bring her body under control. Her core pulsed, and her nipples strained against the silky fabric of her bra. Resting her head against his chest, she slid her hands up around his waist. If she left them on his ass, she'd start again.

They stood this way for a few minutes, their breathing slowing. The scent of their desire swirled between them, but Eleanor could think more clearly. His thoughtfulness and consideration sent warmth coursing through her. He could've taken her right then, but he hadn't.

She leaned back to look up at him. He smiled down at her, the passion in his eyes echoing hers. Something inside her shifted. She touched his face as if seeing him for the first time.

"Who are you really, Michael Stevens?"

"I could ask the same of you," he said, his tone somber.

Eleanor smiled, mischief bubbling up inside of her. "I'm the only child of Robert and Donna Radcliffe, born and raised in California. Recently orphaned and retired, I'm starting a new phase of my life that promises to be..."

65

Words failed her. What would her life be from here on out? She'd thought she'd known. At least for the first few months, her plans involved healing, familiarizing herself with her area, and then maybe some travel. Maybe dating, although she hadn't really considered that until meeting Michael and Rodney.

Now? She had no idea.

A soft touch brought her out of her musings, and she focused on Michael's face again. His eyes shone with compassion.

"It will get better."

"Yeah, well, right now, it's hard."

"I know."

"How do you know? Weren't you born to this?" she asked.

"Yes, and no. My family has been guardians of our land for two generations. Of each generation, there has been one of us in charge of the ley lines."

He released her, and, taking her hands in his, he led her to the porch swing in the corner and sat. She snuggled next to him, resting her head on his shoulder. He draped his arm around her shoulder. A contented sigh escaped her. How long had it been since she'd been held by a man, platonic or otherwise? One? Two? Three years? Since before her parents' illnesses. Between taking care of her dying parents and working, there'd been no time.

Resting her hand on his chest, she closed her eyes and breathed in his clean, spicy scent. Tingles of desire prickled along her skin, and she shivered. She opened her eyes, determined to continue their conversation.

"Who decides who'll be a guardian?"

"The land decides."

His deep voice rumbled through her. She shivered again.

He tightened his arm around her and asked, "Are you cold?"

Not bothering to hide her desire, she looked up at him and smiled. "No."

"If you keep looking at me like that..." Need swirled in his eyes.

Heat pooled inside her. She wanted to kiss him, but if

she did, she wouldn't stop. Glancing away, she took a deep breath and groaned as she inhaled his scent again. She shifted slightly away from him and put her hands in her lap. She had to focus. Focus on something other than what her body wanted.

"So, the land decides? That sounds rather, um..."

"New Age-y," he said.

She nodded, refusing to look at him. *Stay focused.*

"It's true, though. Each generation a guardian is born."

"But aren't you the oldest? What if you hadn't been born?" she asked.

He shrugged. "Yes. I don't know."

He pulled away. She turned to him to see why.

"What?"

Wariness flitted across his features before disappearing. "How did you know I'm the oldest?"

"I...you told me?" she said, confused. Hadn't he told her he was the oldest?

"No. I told you I had brothers."

"Oh...hm... I thought you had. A good guess?"

"Maybe."

The look he gave her set her hair on end.

An uneasy silence settled between them. The camaraderie of moments before vanished. Something odd had just happened. Fear slithered through her body and clawed its way out of the place she had buried it. She rubbed her arms, the chill sinking in once more. The overwhelming urge to escape pressed in on her. She jumped up.

"Well, I'm going to go in." Her voice as chilly as the air, she strode toward the house. "Maybe Angela can use some help with setting up for lunch."

"Eleanor, wait." His footsteps crossed to her.

She stopped. He touched her shoulder.

"We need to talk about this. There's more you need to know."

Unable to bring herself to turn around, she shook her head and said, "No, I can't. I'm... I'm... I'm sorry, but I can't."

Chapter Thirteen

After lunch, Eleanor, Lily, and Angela retreated to a spacious living room. Pale afternoon winter sun filtered in through the large windows. Outside, the beautiful scrub oak reached to the clear, blue sky. A couch faced the windows and stretched the length of one wall.

"Why don't we sit here?" Angela said, motioning to the couch.

Sitting in the center of the couch, Angela unrolled a map of Sedona she'd brought into the room and placed it on a large wooden coffee table in front of the sofa. At each corner, she set a crystal coaster. Eleanor sat next to her and leaned forward to study the map. Lines crisscrossed the map in a matrix. Some were larger and longer than others. Different colored dots marked each intersection of the lines. At some points, there were spirals. In all, eight spirals marked the map.

Eleanor pointed to a spiral. "What are these?"

"Those are vortexes." Angela traced a finger down one of the larger lines. "See how large this ley line is?"

Eleanor nodded.

Angela traced another line until the two lines met. "As you can see when this other major ley line crosses it, there is a vortex. Here the electromagnetic energy of the earth is intensified and, like a vortex, you can feel it swirling up from the earth. It's not like a whirlpool or that strong, but more of a subtle shift."

"You can actually feel it?" Eleanor asked.

"Oh, yes," Lily said. "It's quite amazing. You must visit one of these vortexes sometime, but perhaps not today."

Angela smiled. "Yes, we have other plans for today."

"So, why the map?"

"Well, I wanted to show the ley lines of Sedona to familiarize you with them. These lines encompass the entire earth. They connect one side of the earth to the other. Some are longer than others, as you can see."

"And some go right off the map."

The sound of Michael's voice sent shivers up her spine.

Angela looked up. "Ah, are you going to join us?"

"For a little bit," he said.

Angela turned back to the coffee table, pointing at different spots on it and talking, but Eleanor didn't hear her. Even though she stared at the map, her focus had shifted to Michael. His presence filled the room, and, despite him sitting in a chair a few feet away, his scent seemed to whirl about her, drawing her into a daydream.

The house and Angela and Lily disappeared. Michael and Eleanor stood at the top of a mountain. Sedona spread out below them. His arm encircled her waist, and her hand rested on his chest. Desire flared inside of her, curling in her stomach and spreading through her. She raised her head and gazed into his eyes. An answering flame leapt in his. He lowered his head towards hers.

Closing her eyes, she leaned into him. Their lips met, and she sighed at the soft touch, wanting more. His tongue teased her lips and slid inside her mouth. Sparks of electricity danced through her veins, setting all of her hairs on end. A gasping moan escaped her as she lost herself in the wonder of his kiss.

He caressed her arms, slipped his hands down to the hem of her shirt, and tugged upwards. She raised her arms. Cool air teased her overheated skin, and she shivered.

"Eleanor?"

Angela's voice came from a distance.

Eleanor blinked, the room shimmering in front of her. Her gaze met Angela's. Heat rushed to her cheeks at being caught fantasizing. "I'm sorry. I'm afraid I wasn't paying attention." Her focus flitted to Michael.

Hunger glinted in his eyes. Did he know what she'd been thinking? Her cheeks burned, and she glanced away.

Standing, she said, "I think I need to use the restroom. Would that be okay?"

"Of course. You remember where it is?" Angela asked.

Eleanor nodded and headed to the bathroom.

When she returned, much to her relief, and, if she'd admit it, chagrin, Michael had left. Only Angela and Lily waited for her. They turned as she entered the room.

"Join us. We might as well begin your training," Angela said. "You'll need to be able to focus for this to work. Do you think you can do that?"

Eleanor nodded, but highly doubted she was telling the truth. Too much had happened in the last few weeks for her to be able to focus successfully on anything...except, perhaps Michael.

"Are you sure?" Lily asked. "What you're about to learn can be dangerous if your attention is scattered. Do you need some time to compose yourself?"

Shaking her head, Eleanor took a deep breath and banished all thoughts of Michael from her mind. "Okay. I'm ready."

"Take a deep breath," Janice said. "As you inhale, visualize a white light pouring in through the top of your head and reaching all the way to your toes and through the soles of your feet and into the earth.

"Focus on that breath and light. See it spinning deeper and deeper into the ground, connecting with the earth energy and comingling. As you exhale, see this new combined energy come up through your feet to your shins and knees up through your thighs. See it go up through your hips and your torso until it fills your entire body and pours out through the top of your head and you are a column of this energy.

"With each breath you take, you grow more and more relaxed and your mind calms and is empty of all but your breathing."

Janice's instructions sounded like every meditation technique Eleanor had ever heard. She'd never been that successful at meditation. With a sigh, she breathed deeply and pictured the light pouring through her. She exhaled and imagined the tension and stress leaving her. Her shoulders relaxed, and her breathing deepened.

"Now, open your eyes. Envision a place you'd like to go. A beach, a forest, a garden, any place," Janice said. "See it as if you're there. What does it smell like? What would you hear? Is it warm? Cold? You must create it as if you are there."

Where would she like to be? A memory of her parents' garden filtered through her mind. The smell of damp earth right after the sprinklers ran; the bees buzzing around the rosemary bush; a soft breeze soughing through the trees. Green grass stretched all the way to the trees in the back.

The air shimmered in front of her. Through a misty veil, the garden appeared. Eleanor leaned forward, her eyes widening. Beside her, Lily and Janice gasped, and her focus disintegrated. Thoughts of the Gehglers intruded. The garden whirled into a black hole, and dark, bottomless eyes stared out at her.

"Eleanor." The sibilant whisper slithered through the portal. It reached a clawed hand through the opening. "Come to me."

Eleanor stood and took a step toward it.

"No," Lily shouted and grabbed Eleanor's arm.

Startled, Eleanor jumped and lost focus. The portal disappeared, taking the creature with it.

"You must control your thoughts," Lily said.

Unable to speak, she nodded. If Lily hadn't grabbed her... A pit formed in her stomach. She swallowed and vowed to manage her thoughts better.

* * * *

Over the next four hours, Angela and Lily helped Eleanor begin the process of learning to control her thoughts and her powers. While Eleanor still had a lot to learn, she wouldn't be accidentally using the ley lines for travel anymore or bringing Gehglers to her...she hoped.

Training ended right before dinner. Exhausted after hours of focusing and exploring her newfound abilities, Eleanor craved food, a hot shower, solitude, and sleep.

"How are you feeling?" Angela asked. Her brown eyes studied Eleanor.

Eleanor smiled. "Do I look as tired as I feel? That was grueling."

"I was tired long before you were," Lily said. "I'm amazed you lasted as long as you did."

"But it was a good session—an important session." Angela kneaded the small of her back. "It's a good thing I have some leftovers in the fridge." She stood. "It'll take about a half hour to get things together."

"Do you mind if I shower?" Eleanor asked. "Maybe that will pep me up...at least long enough to eat before I crash."

"Of course. Lily," Angela turned to the quiet, blonde woman, "could you get Eleanor a towel and anything else she may need? Once I get dinner heating, I'll grab you some clean clothes."

"Thank you." Eleanor stood and stretched out the aches of stiff muscles from sitting too long. Yawning, she blinked and walked out of the room and down the hall to the bathroom.

Not only could she lie down in the sunken bathtub, but it had jets. They'd sooth her aching body. No. She'd better shower. If she lay down, she'd fall asleep. With a sigh, she leaned over to turn the shower on, adjusting the temperature.

"Here you go."

Eleanor jumped at the sound of Lily's voice. She looked over her shoulder at her friend and neighbor before facing her. Dark smudges under her eyes attested to Lily's fatigue. Eleanor imagined she looked the same. In her hand, Lily held a towel.

"I'll leave this on the counter. Angela will bring fresh clothes in soon."

"Thank you."

"You are most welcome." She gave Eleanor a tired smile. "It's been a long couple of days."

"Yes, it has."

Lily touched her hand. "It will get better. It does. The beginning is the hardest."

"I hope so." Although still present, the fear had abated some...until she thought of the Gehglers and those solid, black eyes. She shuddered.

Lily squeezed her hand. "They won't get you. We won't let them."

"How did you know?"

"That you were thinking of them? After what happened earlier today and last night, I'm not surprised. It haunts me, too. You're safe here. Now, you shower, and we'll eat." She walked to the door.

"Lily?"

72

She paused, hand on the doorknob, and looked back.

"Thank you—for everything," Eleanor said.

"I'm glad I was there to help."

"Me, too... Me, too."

The door clicked shut behind Lily, and Eleanor shivered. Determined to enjoy her shower, she banished thoughts of Gehglers and ley lines from her mind. Undressing, she stepped into the shower and allowed the water to wash away the tension of the past few days.

Chapter Fourteen

After a long, dreamless night, Eleanor woke refreshed. The aroma of bacon wafted into her bedroom, and her stomach gurgled. If she continued to eat as well as she had yesterday, she wouldn't be able to fit into her clothes. She stretched and smiled. How did Angela do it?

Sitting up, she swung her legs over the edge of the bed and rose. Someone had folded and left her laundered clothes on the dresser. Her stomach grumbled again, urging her to dress quickly and follow the delicious scent teasing her nose.

In the kitchen, everyone sat around the table, except Angela, who set a heaping plate of bacon on the table before returning to the stove. She pulled a plate of scrambled eggs out of the oven and handed them to Eleanor.

"Could you put those on the table for me?" she asked.

"Of course." Eleanor set the plate down and said, "Is there anything else I can do?"

"Please sit and help yourself," Angela said.

At that moment, Eleanor felt like she could eat the entire plate. She pulled out a chair and said, "It looks wonderful, Angela. Thank you."

"My pleasure." Angela smiled. "With my kids grown and my husband away, I miss not having a crew to cook for."

"Well, I can honestly say I'm enjoying the break." Lily grabbed a couple pieces of bacon and spooned some eggs onto her plate. "When I get home, I'll be feeding my brood again. Not that I mind. It's just nice to have someone else do it every so often." She handed the plate of eggs to Eleanor. "You better dig in before it's all gone. From the sounds of your stomach, you're hungry."

Laughter filled the air, and conversation flowed. Eleanor had never enjoyed a group of people as much as she did these three, not even her family. Their conversations consisted of who had done what and what they would've done if it had happened to them. They meant well, but she always imagined them judging her and finding her deficient.

"Is there anything you'd like me to give to Michael to bring back from your house, besides a suitcase of clothes and your toiletries?" Lily asked. "I leave for the airport soon. I can pack it up and send it back with Michael."

Surprised, Eleanor looked at the man who commandeered too much of her attention and asked, "Oh, are you accompanying Lily?" She thought he was staying a few more days. Disappointment seeped into her.

He nodded and looked away. "I need to check on a few things back at the ranch. My younger brother, Garth, called this morning. Some cattle have gone missing."

A gasp escaped Eleanor. "Do you think it's the Gehglers?"

"Could be. Could be a puma. Could be rustlers. Could be any number of things. This is the kind of stuff I usually deal with. Garth's still in school. He doesn't have the time or the experience, especially if it's Gehglers."

"Well, I hope it's not them," Lily said.

"Me, too," Angela said. "It'd require calling a meeting of the keepers."

"We won't know until Michael returns. In the meantime, is there anything else you'd like me to bring?" Lily asked.

Eleanor took a bite of her scrambled eggs. *Was there anything she cared about there?* She chewed, considering the contents of her house. Very few of her belongings meant something to her. Her mother had insisted on purging "unnecessary dust collectors" once a year. As a result, she'd learned not to form attachments to most material things. It was the reason her house was so Spartan. The only things she cared about were the family photos and her mother's jewelry box.

She swallowed before saying, "Can you check on my storage bins in the garage? There are two full of family photos. Maybe we should move them for the time being. Do you think the creatures would destroy them?"

"You never know with the Gehglers," Angela said. She picked up her plate and carried it to the sink. Washing it, she continued. "If they think it may have some value to you and they are angry, they can be very vindictive."

A pit formed in Eleanor's stomach. If she lost those photos... "So, my house could be trashed, the photos

75

destroyed?"

Lily reached for Eleanor's hand and nodded. "It's possible."

Sucking in a deep breath, she steadied herself. If necessary, she could ask her relatives for copies of photos. Of course, they'd use it as leverage to try to reel her back to their side. Having tasted freedom, if only for a short time, she wanted to keep it.

"If you see anything else you think I might want, please either put it in storage or send it to me here. The photos should go to an air-conditioned storage. Of course, just about anywhere the Gehglers can't access them would be good. The only other thing I care about is my mother's jewelry box. There is nothing of true value in there, just sentimental, but I'd still like to have it." If those creatures had taken or destroyed her mother's wedding ring, her grandmother's cameo, and the locket with the lock of her baby hair, she didn't know what she'd do.

A sob caught in her throat. She couldn't lose those, too.

"Hey."

Michael's warm, chocolaty voice drew out of her thoughts. She glanced up. He squeezed her shoulder. Compassion filled his eyes.

"We don't know yet what shape your house and its contents are in. As my mother always said, 'Don't borrow trouble.'"

She released a breath she didn't realize she'd been holding and turned a wobbly smile on him. "You're right. It's just so much has happened in the past couple of weeks. Not just weeks, these past couple of years. It's..."

He pulled her up into his embrace. She clung to him. Leaning into him, she breathed in his scent. It swirled around her. Her heartbeat slowed, and peace settled upon her. She would stay in his arms forever if she could. He had to go home and check on his ranch. She had to train to learn the ley lines and how to protect herself.

She stepped back and looked into his eyes. "Thank you."

He tucked a curl behind her ear and smiled. "Any time."

"When will you be back?" she asked Michael.

"In a few days."

76

With a reluctant sigh, she stepped out of his embrace. "Oh, well, I'll need to go shopping, won't I?" She couldn't wear borrowed clothes for much longer.

"We can do that after we drop them at the airport. It won't take long. There aren't many clothing shops in Sedona," Angela said.

"And they are...unique," Lily added with a grin.

Angela laughed. "One could say that."

"What does that mean?" Eleanor had never cared much about clothes. She wore what was expected of her for work and hadn't really deviated from the conservative look in her personal life.

"You'll look good whatever you wear. Don't worry about them," Michael said.

Lily nudged Eleanor and winked. "From a man who's obviously smitten."

He raised his hands in surrender, a twinkle in his eye. "I am completely unbiased."

"Uh-huh," Lily said.

"Well, guys, I hate to break up the party, but we need to finish breakfast and get you two to the airport." Angela shook her finger at them. "So, less talking more eating."

Laughter filled the air, followed by silence as everyone did as told. Soon, plates were emptied and in the dishwasher, and the group was filing out to the car.

Ten minutes later, Angela and Eleanor dropped Michael and Lily off at the airport and were headed to downtown Sedona to buy some clothes. After searching three shops, Eleanor found a few items. Not her style—New Age, flowing, and not remotely conservative, they would serve their purpose until her regular clothes arrived. They also picked up some underwear.

Back at Angela's house, Eleanor asked as they walked into the kitchen, "Do you mind if I use your phone to get my messages?"

"Of course not." Angela retrieved the cordless phone from the counter and gave it to her. She picked up the bag full of clothes. "I'm going to throw these in the washing machine. I'll be back in a few minutes."

"Thanks," Eleanor said and dialed her home number.

"You have three new voice messages," the machine said. "Press one to play first new voice message."

She pressed one and waited.

"First new message recorded Saturday at ten thirteen a.m."

"Hey, girlfriend." Eleanor smiled at the sound of Jennifer's bubbly voice. "Just calling to find out how you are doing and what happened with the sheriff. I haven't heard from you. Call me. I've got some news... Good news."

"End of first new voice message. Press two to save message. Press three to replay message. Press four to hear next message. Press seven to delete message."

Eleanor punched in four.

"Second new voice message recorded Saturday at twelve twenty-two p.m."

"Eleanor?" Rodney's deep voice, edged with worry, filled the line. "Are you there? I stopped by Lily's house, and no one was home. The front bushes were destroyed and there are deep gouge marks on the front door. I'm going to your house now. Please call me when you get the chance."

When she finished listening to all of her messages, she'd ask Angela how to contact Lily. They needed to warn her just in case the creatures waited for her.

"Press two to save message. Press three to replay message. Press four to hear next message. Press seven to delete message."

Again, Eleanor pressed four.

"Third new message recorded Saturday at twelve thirty-three p.m."

"Eleanor, it's Rodney again. I'm at your house. The front door is open. I hope you don't mind that I've gone inside."

Eleanor grabbed the back of the chair. Her stomach muscles clenched. No one should be in her house right now, not even a sheriff.

"Your couch has been slashed, and there are small handprints all over the place. Your bedroom door is closed..."

Leave, Rodney. Leave.

"I'm going to...what the—shit!"

The sound of gunshots followed by a loud snarl and screaming zipped through the phone line before it went dead. Eleanor gasped. Panic threatened to overwhelm her. Her face tingled, and she swayed. Hands shaking, she stared at the phone.

Chapter Fifteen

"Eleanor? Eleanor? What is it?"

Angela's voice broke through the horror gripping Eleanor. "You need to listen to this." She pushed three and handed the phone to Angela.

Angela's eyes widened, her face turned pale. She stood silent for a moment. "Although it doesn't sound good, it might not be what it sounds like."

Eleanor looked at her with disbelief, but she didn't respond. Let her new friend and mentor keep her illusions. Her gut told her he'd tangled with the Gehglers. She prayed he'd survived it.

"Have you tried calling him?"

Eleanor shook her head. "No. I just listened to it. I'm... I'm not sure what to do."

"Well, try to call him." The other woman handed her the phone.

"There's more."

"More?"

"Yes, more. We need to get ahold of Lily. They trashed the bushes in the front of her house and put gouges in the door."

The steam seemed to leave Angela. She sank into a chair. "Okay. I'll call the others. Things are escalating much quicker than I thought they would." She stared hard at Eleanor as if trying to figure out a puzzle. "There must be something you aren't telling us. They have never reacted this way before."

"If there is, it's nothing I'm aware of. I've told you everything I know."

"All right. I'll contact Siobhan, David, and Gabriel. Michael will need some back up. There is no question he'll be dealing with the Gehglers. I'll set some extra protection wards around the house. In the meantime, call Rodney. Make sure he's okay." She handed the phone back to Eleanor and left the room.

Eleanor dialed Rodney's phone number. On the third

ring, he answered.

"Hello."

At the sound of his voice, she nearly collapsed into the chair in relief. "Thank God you're okay."

"Eleanor? Is that you?"

"Yes, it is. I'm sorry I didn't respond to your earlier call."

"Where are you?"

Something about his voice set her on edge. "I'm out of town. It got pretty scary that night as you can tell by the bushes, but we survived. Lily thought it might be better for me to leave for a few days. I'm staying with a friend."

"Oh, that's too bad. I was hoping to see you tonight."

"Not tonight. I called to make sure you were okay. What happened?"

"Nothing really."

All of the hair on her body stood on end. Something was wrong. Seriously wrong. "But I heard gunshots and screaming."

"Oh, those. It was just a coyote that scared me." He paused. "Where are you? When will you be home?"

"I'm not sure." Loath to lie to him, she kept it vague. "Just a friend's."

"Why won't you tell me where you are?" His voice deepened to a guttural snarl. "I need to know."

Unease spread through her, and she shivered. She had to end this conversation quickly. "I'm sorry I—I hear someone calling me. I can't talk any longer."

She hung up and then realized that if he looked at the caller ID, he'd see the area code and be able to track her. Why had she deactivated her cell phone? Because she didn't want to be on call every hour of the day. Because, if she'd kept her cell phone, her family would have called her on the hour, every hour. With only a landline, she felt less accessible. Now, she rued her decision.

The phone rang. Caller ID identified it as Rodney Tyler.

Shit. She let the phone ring. It wouldn't do any good. Now he knew where she was. She might as well answer it.

"Hello."

"Eleanor. That wasn't very nice to hang up." His voice came out in a sibilant whisper. "You cannot hide from me. I will find you."

"I'm not trying to." She had to get him off the phone and tell Angela. They couldn't stay here.

Angela entered the room. "Is everything okay?"

She shook her head, put a finger to her lips, and pointed to the phone.

"Who're you talking to, Eleanor? Is that Angela? Tell her that Esme said, 'Hello.'"

"Esme?"

Angela's face blanched. "Esme?" Her voice broke on the name. "Oh, God."

"Now, you just wait there. I'm coming to get you."

The line went dead.

Angela grabbed her arm. "We have to leave. Now. I'll call and leave a message for Michael and Lily."

"What about my clothes?"

"We don't have time." She rushed to the closet and pulled out a couple of jackets. "Here, you'll need this." She pulled out her cellphone and dialed. "Hi, Michael, this is Angela. We've had a change of plans. We've got to leave here. I'll call you when we arrive. Be careful and please warn Lily. The Gehglers have Esme." She turned to Eleanor. "Okay. Let's go."

"Where are we going?"

"To the Cathedral Rock vortex. It's very popular. With all of the different energies there, it'll be harder for them to track us." Angela grabbed her purse and her keys and strode toward the door. "We don't have much time."

Eleanor rushed to catch up. "Who is Esme?"

"Esme is an ally of the Gehglers." She unlocked the car, and the two climbed in. "Sometimes, she makes mischief, but, most of the time, she doesn't involve herself in this type thing. Only if it's something big." She stared hard at Eleanor before turning on the car. "What don't we know about you?" She shook her head. "I don't have time to figure it out right now. We've got to go."

On the way to the rock, Angela made another call. "Hi, Pat. Would you mind meeting me at Crescent Moon Park? I have to leave town suddenly and was wondering if you and Jerry could pick up my car for me... Great, I'll see you there."

"Do they know about...this?"

Angela nodded. "Yes. They're not keepers, but they're aware of the travelers. It's hard to live in Sedona and not be."

A few minutes later, they pulled up to a park. Angela held up her park pass as they passed the ranger booth. He smiled at her and motioned for her to go in. A couple of tour busses and some cars occupied most of the parking lot. Beyond the busses, an older couple stood next to a car and smiled. Angela's car came to a stop beside them.

The two women got out of the car. Eleanor wiped her damp palms on her borrowed jeans. Meeting new people always made her nervous.

A woman stepped forward. Her long, gray-streaked brown hair flowed over her shoulders and down her woven jacket. Kind blue eyes studied Eleanor. A man stood behind her. His keen hazel eyes took everything in. Calm radiated off of them, and Eleanor relaxed under their friendly scrutiny.

"I see you have a new traveler with you, Angela."

"I do. Pat, Jerry, this is Eleanor. Eleanor, this is Pat and her husband Jerry. We've been friends for a long time."

They shook hands.

"It's a pleasure to meet you," Eleanor said.

"We always enjoy meeting Angela's friends," Pat replied. "So, what can we do for you?"

"Just take my car back to your house, if you don't mind."

Surprise flitted across Pat's face. "*Our* house?"

Angela nodded. "Yes, your house. There are some uninvited guests arriving shortly at my house. I don't want anyone there. It's not safe. The house is protected by wards, but I want them to see the car is gone. Hopefully, they'll think we drove somewhere instead of traveling the ley lines." She returned to the car and grabbed two canteens, handing one to Eleanor, who looked at her questioningly. "It's not that long of a hike, but it's always best to be prepared."

"Thanks," Eleanor said.

A woman in a jogging suit walked by with her dog and nodded to them.

"Hi, Dana, is it busy today?" Angela asked her.

"Like always, Angela. There's a group of tourists coming back and another on their way up. If you're looking to go somewhere, you'll find it a bit busy."

"Thanks. We'll manage." She turned back to the couple, handing the keys to Pat. "I'd like to get going, if that's okay."

Pat smiled. "Of course. Call us when you want us to bring the car back."

"I will. Again, thank you."

The couple hugged Angela.

"We'll see you soon," Pat said. She nodded to Eleanor. "It was a pleasure to meet you. Hopefully, we'll see you again."

Angela turned to Eleanor. "I hadn't planned on testing your new skills so soon, but I think you'll be okay." When Eleanor didn't respond, Angela patted her shoulder. "You'll be fine." She looked up the path. "I need to send a text before we go up the trail. It will only take a second." She tapped out a message, then shut off her phone and stuffed it in her pocket. "Ready. Well, we best get going. The longer we linger, the stronger the residue of our energy becomes."

They turned up the path. Cathedral Rock towered over them, orange and yellow striations marked its vibrant red rock. Along one side of the path, oak trees grew. Along the other, Oak Creek burbled. Red dirt swirled under their feet in small puffs. The further away from the parking lot they hiked, the more peaceful it became, the sounds of nature encompassing them.

Eleanor drew in a deep breath and exhaled. The tension from the last hour drained from her body. Energy flowed around them, increasing with each step they took. By the time they reached the vortex, her body hummed with it. Even the two busloads of people wandering the area, their conversations muted in the sacred place, didn't dampen the feeling of peace that stole over her.

"It's amazing, isn't it?" Angela asked in a hushed tone.

Unable to speak, she nodded. Nothing could truly describe what she was experiencing.

"Come. We must find a secluded spot to do this," Angela said.

"Is it best to be right where the vortex is?"

"It's easier, but not necessary at this point. It's too busy to worry about that. We don't have time to wait for people to leave. They'll be coming and going all day."

A large crowd passed by them, their tour guide leading them down the path back toward the parking lot.

"Well, that helped some," Angela said. "Let's go over there."

They walked over to an area where only a few people were exploring. Just beyond the tourists, the creek widened, and a small eddy swirled by the riverbank. Angela walked toward the eddy. Eleanor followed. Energy skittered along her skin, and goose bumps trailed in its wake.

Eleanor shivered. "Wow. This is intense."

Angela smiled at her. "Yes, it is, especially the first time you experience it consciously."

"How do we open—"

The air stirred in front of them and then wavered like heat rising from pavement. The waves extended from the ground to a foot above their heads.

Angela grabbed her arm and pulled her toward the trees. "Not here. People will see." She stopped behind a large oak.

"What was that?" Eleanor motioned back toward the stream.

"You were opening a portal."

"Really?" She hadn't done any of the techniques the other woman had showed her. "How? I thought I had to focus."

"You didn't?"

"No," Eleanor said, "I just asked the question."

The look Angela gave her sent unease shooting through her.

"All right. We're headed for another keeper's house. It's in San Antonio. Have you been to San Antonio?" Angela asked.

She shook her head. "No."

"Well, I want you just to focus on the name of the town and state, then. Let's see what happens."

Eleanor did as instructed. The air wavered in front of them again. Beyond the portal, a cobblestone plaza crowded with people and a limestone block building with the famous Alamo arches shimmered. Stunned, she just stared. Was it a mirage? Surely, she was imagining it. Despite her training and the happenings of the past few days, all of this held a tinge of the impossible.

A gasp escaped the woman standing beside her. "Amazing," she whispered. She touched Eleanor's arm. "Ready?"

Unable to speak, she nodded. Was she ready? Did she have a choice?

Angela took Eleanor's limp hand and stepped into the rift, pulling her along. A rush of intoxicating energy swept over Eleanor. She quivered, and then it was gone. They stood in the square outside of the Alamo. She stumbled when someone bumped into her.

"Now, where did you come from?" a man's voice said from behind them.

"You must've been looking somewhere else. We've been here for the last few minutes," Angela said.

He regarded them with a doubtful expression. "I—"

"Come on, Daddy," a little, blond boy with bright blue eyes said. "Let's go." The boy grabbed his daddy's hand and pulled him toward the long line that wrapped around the side of the famous landmark. "We'll never get in if we don't get in line."

The man watched the two women from over his shoulder for a few minutes before the crowd swallowed him and his son.

"That was close. Next time, choose somewhere less crowded."

Eleanor looked at Angela in disbelief. "I've never been to San Antonio. You asked me to focus on it. The only place I could think of was the Alamo. Perhaps next time *you* should do it."

Angela shook her head and started walking down a street. "No. You need to practice, especially now that we're on the run."

On the run. How had her life devolved into this?

Chapter Sixteen

By noon, they were settled in at the new location. The two women sat at the kitchen table while another keeper, Heather, made them all sandwiches. Heather had picked them up in front of the Rivercenter Mall where Angela and Eleanor had shopped for a few necessities, a few changes of clothing, and carryon luggage while waiting for her to arrive. Eleanor bought a prepaid cell phone. She'd learned her lesson. No one would be able to track her. If they were lucky, they'd be able to stay for a few days before moving on to the next keeper.

"We appreciate you allowing us to stay here for a few days, Heather," Angela said.

Heather smiled, but concern lit her brown eyes. She tucked a strand of long brown hair behind an ear. "I'm happy to have some company. Although, after hearing about your experiences," she nodded at Eleanor, "it's imperative that we keep you safe." She set down two plates with sandwiches on them in front of Angela and Eleanor. Grabbing a third from the counter, she put it in front of another chair at the table. "What would you like to drink? I have water, hot tea, and diet soda."

"Hot tea sounds lovely," Eleanor said, rubbing her hands together. Despite the half hour car ride, she hadn't been able to dispel the chill that had settled on her since stepping out at the Alamo.

Angela touched Eleanor's arm. "Your body will adapt. It takes a lot of energy to travel the ley lines, especially in the beginning. More training will help you expend less energy. Which reminds me, we need to get some training in today." She turned to Heather. "You don't mind if we focus on that while we're here, do you?"

"No," the other woman said, "We need to contact the other keepers, let them know Esme is involved. While you train her, I'll make some calls. I also have work to do."

"Great."

They finished their lunch in silence. All of the happenings of the previous days swirled in Eleanor's head. Nearly overwhelmed with everything, she focused on breathing and eating. In the days to come, she knew she'd need her strength.

After lunch, they began another session of training. She worked to control her focus, to open portals, and to still her mind. This took up the rest of the day with a few bathroom and stretch breaks and dinner. That evening in her bedroom, she called her friend Jennifer using her new phone.

"Hello." Jennifer's cheerful voice filled the line.

"Hey, Jennifer. It's Eleanor. How are you?"

"I'm good, but where have you been? I've left several messages for you, so has your family. I've been worried about you. A sheriff named Officer Tyler called asking about you. He said you'd gone missing. When we didn't hear back from you, your family filed a missing person's report on you."

A chill ran down Eleanor's spine, followed by anger. She was an adult. She didn't need to check in to go away, even if she really was on the run. "I went away for a few days and because no one heard from me, they think I've gone missing? Since when did I need to run my itinerary by anyone?"

"From what Officer Tyler said—"

"Officer Tyler was a guy who asked me out and I decided not to date. I left to get away from him." It was a lie, but Jennifer didn't need to know that he was possessed.

"He didn't sound that way at all. He called on official sheriff business."

"Official sheriff's business?"

"Your house was ransacked, and you were gone without a trace."

"Well, the house was ransacked after I left. Who's to say who did it? I spoke to him yesterday. He threatened me."

"What? Oh, Eleanor, I didn't know. I'm sorry. You should call your family. They've been worried sick."

She sighed. The last thing she wanted to do was call her family. They'd blow this out of proportion. Then she started laughing. Out of proportion? Hysteria bubbled up inside of her. A possessed sheriff had convinced her family she was missing, Gehglers were chasing her, perhaps to possess her

88

as well, or eat her, whichever took their fancy, and she was worried that her family would blow this out of proportion? She laughed so hard tears ran down her cheeks.

"Eleanor? Are you okay?" Jennifer's concerned voice sobered her a little.

Taking a deep breath, she wiped her eyes on her sleeve. Another giggle escaped her before she could answer. "I'm sorry. If you only knew..." She giggled again. "Ah... I'm fine. It's just been a rough few days, Jen."

The giggles eased the tension that had been gripping her. She'd have to call her aunt and let her know everything was fine and to cancel the missing person report. Angela needed to be informed, as did Michael and Lily. They knew about Rodney, but not about this. If only Michael were there...she wanted his arms around her.

"I can tell," Jennifer said. "Well, I'm glad you're okay. Just call your aunt."

"I will. I promise."

"When will you be home?"

"I don't know. It could be a few weeks yet. I'll keep you updated."

"Okay. I miss you, girlfriend. I wish you'd never moved."

Melancholy seeped into Eleanor. "I miss you, too, Jen."

"Call me, please."

"I will."

An awkward silence settled between them.

"Okay, I better call my aunt," Eleanor said. "I'll talk to you again, soon."

"All right. Bye."

"Bye."

Eleanor hung up and stared unseeing out the window. What was she going to tell her aunt? She didn't want to call her. It'd require more lies.

Turning from the window, she sat on the bed and leaned forward, resting her head on her hands. Her aunt would interrogate her, tell her she'd made a mistake moving, and order her to move back to San Jose. Her family would take care of her. Eleanor shuddered at the thought. She loved her family, but they'd direct her life, in a well-meaning way, of course. They'd disapprove of Michael and Lily and would never understand her abilities.

She snorted. As if she could ever tell them about her abilities. One word about them, and her entire family would pray for her salvation. No, first, they'd set up an exorcism. If that didn't work, they'd have her committed. All the while telling their friends how they'd known something was wrong with her since her birth.

Another sigh slipped from her, and she looked up. Procrastinating wouldn't change anything.

She dialed her aunt's number and waited.

"Hello?"

"Hi, Aunt Shirley."

"Eleanor? Oh, my God, it's really you, Eleanor?" A sob cut her aunt short.

"Yes, it is. I'm sorry I didn't call sooner, but I wasn't aware there was an issue."

"Not an issue?" Her aunt's voice rose. "Your house is torn apart, you disappear, a sheriff calls us, and you don't see an issue? This is so typical of you, Eleanor. You never think of anyone but yourself."

"Aunt Shirley, I'm sorry I didn't call sooner. I had no idea all of this was going on." She gave her aunt the same story she'd told Jennifer.

"Well, it figures you'd get yourself into a mess like this, Ellie. If I'd known about Officer Tyler...but then how was I to know since you never call us."

"There was no way for you to know. It's okay. I'm safe, and I'll keep you updated, okay?"

"All right, but you'd be much better off here in San Jose than that godforsaken place you moved to."

"I know. Don't worry. I'll be fine." *Famous last words*, Eleanor thought. "Look, I've got to get going. I love you."

"Hmph."

"You'll cancel the missing person's report?"

"Oh, yes, of course. As soon as I get off the phone with you."

"Thanks. Talk to you soon."

"Uh-huh. Bye-bye."

"Bye."

Exhausted, Eleanor slumped into the chair. God, she

just wanted all of it to end. If only she had never moved to that house, none of this would've happened. But, then, she'd still be under her family's thumb, her choices restricted. In San Jose, a family member stopped by nearly every day to check on her. They meant well, but, for someone like her who enjoyed her solitude, it grated after a time. One day without someone asking her if she was okay would've been nice. Their constant hovering suffocated her. She'd had to escape. The Fresno house had seemed like the perfect solution. Far enough away, they couldn't drop by, but close enough for her to visit them if she felt like it.

"Ugh," she said, "what a mess."

With a sigh, she stood. Rehashing the past and her choices wouldn't change the present, or tomorrow for that matter. One thing at a time. That's what she had to do.

Grabbing the towel Heather had left draped over the chair, Eleanor gathered her nightclothes and headed for the bathroom. A shower would relax her. No baths. She might fall asleep again, and God only knew what she'd summon this time...although she wouldn't mind a repeat with Michael.

No. She shook her head. Besides, he was a distraction, one she didn't need at the moment as much as she wanted him.

My family would disapprove anyway.

With a huff, she shut the bathroom door. How would they know? And why did she still care? She snorted. Who was she kidding? As liberating as the past weeks had been, she couldn't change that quickly. But she was going to change. A determination to be the woman she dreamed of being, knew existed somewhere beneath all the layers of protection and fear, unfurled inside of her. Even in this dark moment, hope shone bright, and she hummed as she took her shower.

Chapter Seventeen

Out in the garden, Tomani waited. She could see him under the oak tree. He'd come every day at this time for the past three days, blending in with the bark and leaves. Tomani was funny and made her laugh. Yesterday, he'd given her a beautiful necklace. The stone with a carved unicorn that shimmered and glowed rainbow colors hung from a silver chain. She loved unicorns.

"Never take it off. Wear it always," he'd said.

"I will," she promised.

Of course, she'd taken it off for her bath last night and tucked it into her nightstand, but as soon as her mommy put her to bed, she'd retrieved it and put it on. It hung around her neck under her shirt, warm against her skin.

The dew on the grass sparkled in the early morning sun. Little Ellie stared longingly out the window and then down at her empty plate. Her mom stood at the kitchen sink cleaning up the breakfast dishes. Ellie stood and carried her dish to the sink, handing it to her mother.

"Mommy, I'm done. Can I go outside now?"

Her mother turned her head and smiled down at her daughter, her chocolate brown eyes soft with love. "Of course. You sure love playing in the garden, Eleanor."

"Uh-huh."

"What do you play every morning?"

"We play—"

"We?" Her mother's eyes widened with alarm, and she grabbed Ellie's arm. "We who?"

"My friend."

Her mother crouched down in front of her. "What friend? You've never told me of a friend before."

"I have. You always smile and nod when I talk about him. He's really nice, Mommy."

The color washed out of her mother's face. "What's his name?" her mom demanded.

"Tomani."

Her mother gasped. "Tomani?" She glanced toward the back door. "He's here?" she said under her breath.

"Mommy?"

She looked down at Ellie and said more forcefully, "He's here now?"

Ellie nodded. "Uh-huh." She pointed to the backyard. "He's waiting under the big tree for me."

Panic-stricken eyes stared out of a terrified face at Ellie. "What has he told you?"

Ellie didn't understand what she meant. "Mommy?"

Her mother took a deep breath and seemed to collect herself. "I mean, what do you do?"

"Most of the time we just play. We talk to the animals and climb the tree. Sometimes, he'll tell me stories."

"About what?"

Panic rimmed her mother's voice again, her eyes dark with concern. Ellie didn't understand the concern. Tomani would never hurt her. He was nice.

"He's told me about his world. He doesn't live here. He's just visiting, he says."

Fear flitted across her mother's face. "Has he taken you there?'"

The little girl shook her head. "No. He said I should never go anywhere without asking you first."

Her mother's shoulders dropped, the tightness around her eyes eased, and she hugged Ellie. "He's right. Now, you stay here, and I'll go talk to Tomani, okay?"

"Are we in trouble, Mommy?"

"No, sugar," she said, gently touching her daughter's face. "Now, I'll be right back. Be a good girl and stay in the house."

"Okay." Ellie watched her mom, worried.

Her mother stood and strode to the back door, opening it as if she feared she'd break it.

Ellie rushed to the window. Mommy said she wasn't mad, but Ellie knew that look and the walk. Tomani stepped out from the tree, smiling. The smile disappeared as her mother approached. Soon, they were arguing. Then Tomani disappeared, and her mother stalked back to the house. When she entered, she smiled at Ellie as if everything *was okay, but Ellie knew everything wasn't okay.*

"Mommy? Where'd Tomani go? Is he not playing with me today?"

Kneeling, her mother looked her in the eye and said, "No. He's left. He won't be coming back. I told him to leave you alone."

Eyes wide, Ellie stared up at her mother. "But why? I don't want him to leave. I like him. He's my friend."

"It's better for you if he never comes back."

She shook her little head in denial. Her attention strayed to the empty space where her friend used to wait for her. "No."

"Look at me, Eleanor. This is for the best. You are safe now," her mother said.

Tears pricked at the back of Ellie's eyes, and her lips trembled. The thought of never seeing Tomani again... She sucked in her lip. Mommy didn't like it when she cried. Struggling to hold back the tears, she stared out the window at the empty garden. He'd never come back. Mommy would see to that.

Ellie blinked, and something inside of her shriveled up and melted away.

* * * *

Eleanor's eyes opened. Darkness surrounded her. Years had passed since that day. The last day she'd seen her best friend. How had she forgotten it? Forgotten him?

"Tomani," she breathed. She reflexively reached for the pendant, but it wasn't there. Not long after that incident, her mother had discovered the necklace and had taken it away from her.

"You don't need this," her mother had said and pocketed it.

She'd been a child, not even six at the time. A few months later, she'd started kindergarten and forgotten about him over time, but she'd never been the same. To this day, she struggled to make friends.

A tear trickled down her cheek, followed by another and another. Her heart contracted with pain, but she took a deep breath and embraced it. She'd run from the pain all of her life. Running hadn't worked.

"I'm so sorry," she whispered. "I didn't know. Oh, Tomani, I miss you."

She sniffled and swiped at the tears. No. She'd denied her feelings for too long. Something had to change. She wrapped her arms around herself and allowed herself to feel again. Anger and sadness mingled, and she let them take over. Her body shook with sobs. She cried for the little girl who'd lost her friend, for the adult who'd kept everyone at bay and hid, and, for the first time, she grieved the loss of her friend and for the child who'd never been the same.

The tears slowed and subsided. Her eyelids drooped, and sleep claimed her.

Chapter Eighteen

Early the next morning, Eleanor awoke with one goal: to find the pendant. Some part of her knew that even if her mother had betrayed her, she hadn't thrown it away. Excitement zipped through her. She knew exactly where her mother had hidden it.

Leaping out of bed, she threw some clothes on and rushed into the kitchen.

Angela sat at the table, a mug of steaming coffee in front of her.

Breathless, she said, "Angela, I've got to go home."

Her mentor's eyes widened. "What? You can't."

"I have to. There's something I have to retrieve."

"Can't Lily or Michael get it for you?" she asked.

The question stopped her for a moment. "I... That's right. I asked Lily to pick up my jewelry box." Had she? "We need to call her. Now." She could almost feel the Gehglers closing in. "Do you have her number?"

"Of course." She pulled her phone out of her pocket and dialed. "Hi, Lily, it's Angela. Have you picked up the jewelry box yet?" There was silence as she waited for the answer. "You haven't had the chance to go over there at all? What about Michael?" Again, she listened to Lily. "I see. Is everyone okay?" The color drained from her face. "Oh, Lily..."

"What's wrong?" Eleanor demanded, her stomach churning with alarm.

Angela waved at her distractedly. "Oh, thank God." She nodded. "Uh-huh...uh-huh... Of course, I understand. You have to take care of your family... Okay. I'll let her know." She turned to Eleanor. "The Gehglers have gone on a spree. They nearly grabbed two of Lily's kids as they walked from the end of driveway to the house on Monday. Only her children saw them. Lily said she just happened to be outside when she heard them screaming. She was able to fend them off, but she's really worried. She's sent them to stay with their grandmother until this all settles down. In the meantime, she's increased the wards and expanded them to the edge of her property, but, until last night, she's heard them snarling and crying outside."

Eleanor's heart thudded. Her skin prickled as fear coursed through her. "It stopped last night?"

"Yes."

She hadn't told Angela and Heather about her dream. Was it a coincidence that the creatures retreated? Or had her dream alerted them to her location? *Get a grip, Eleanor. You're just hypersensitive right now.*

Urgency spread through her. "If she can't do it, I have to."

"It's going to have to wait," Angela said. "It's not safe."

"You don't understand. It can't." She told her about her dream, the pendant, and everything else that had happened during the night. The more she talked, the more intense and serious Angela grew. "I don't know how long it will take for that missing person's report to clear across the country, but I do know that pendant will change things. It calls to me."

The look in her brown eyes grave, the other woman said, "You're right. You need to go back and get it. I'll come with you. Do you know where it is?"

"If it's where I left it, yes."

"It'll be there. They won't touch it. They *can't* touch it. And it's why they want you so much." Angela covered Eleanor's hand with her own and leaned toward her. "Now I get what's going on." She jumped up and grabbed her empty coffee mug. "But we don't have time to discuss it. We've got to move *now*. The Gehglers and Esme are close." She handed her a banana from the fruit bowl and a granola bar from the cupboard. "You'll need this. Eat the banana, then we'll leave."

"I think we should go now."

She shook her head. "No. You need the energy. Eat."

Eleanor ate as quickly as she could.

When she finished, Angela said, "Now, I want you to think of exactly where that pendant is and slowly open a line to it."

Eleanor pictured her bedroom and the dresser against the east wall. The air wavered in front of them. Just beyond the wavering air was her dresser, untouched. The jewelry box sat on top of her dresser. The two women stepped through the hole and into her room. Snarls and keening from the other side of the door greeted them. The door shook but held under the onslaught of child-sized fists.

Panic threatened to overtake her, but Angela squeezed her hand and said, "They can't come in. That pendant is protecting this room."

Wide-eyed, she nodded and drew in a couple of deep breaths. *Ignore them, Eleanor. They can't get you.*

At that thought, everything stopped, and an eerie, pregnant silence engulfed them. Then she heard it—the sibilant whisper of weeks past.

"Eleanor, let me in," it commanded. *"Open the door for us. We need you."*

In a trance, Eleanor stepped toward the door.

A hand on her arm stopped her, and Angela pulled her back. "Don't listen to them. Stay focused. What did you come here for?"

As if wading through a quagmire, she struggled to regain control of her mind and body.

A deep voice from her past that she recognized as Tomani's whispered in her mind, *Tune them out, Leeli. They cannot control you. I cannot help you, but the pendant can. Get the pendant.*

Shivers coursed through her, but she broke free of the mind control. The snarling and pounding on the door resumed. A scream of pure rage pierced the air. Eleanor jumped. *Christ!* Fear slammed into her again.

Calm down, Leeli. They can't get in. You have to let them in. Just don't let them in.

Drawing in a deep breath, she walked calmly to the dresser and grabbed the jewelry box. Unable to stop herself, she clutched it to her breast and turned to Angela.

"I'm ready. Let's go."

"As soon as we're gone, they'll open that door. Is there anything else you want?"

She looked around at her bedroom's sparse furnishings, her dresser, her bed, the bare walls, the matching nightstands and lamps. Nothing had any real meaning for her, except the picture of her parents that sat on the nightstand next to her phone. With quick steps, she crossed the room and grasped her parents' wedding photo. Their happy smiles drew one from her. She gazed at them for a second before returning to Angela.

"Okay. I'm ready."

"No clothes?"

Eleanor shook her head. "No. They can be replaced." Her new life was beginning. The thought of the oncoming destruction angered her, but if she'd learned anything from her parents' deaths it was that everything had a silver lining. This would force her to start anew. She'd remake her life in the image she wanted.

"All right then. Lead on."

"Will they follow us?"

A grim smile graced Angela's face, her eyes sparkled with satisfaction. "They won't be able to. That pendant will obscure our energies. Now, open the ley line and let's be gone."

Visualizing Heather's kitchen, Eleanor opened a portal, and they stepped through to safety.

Chapter Nineteen

Bright and airy, and infused with Heather's joyful presence, the lightness of the kitchen's energy welcomed them back, the oppressive aura of her house only apparent now that they'd left it. Eleanor breathed a sigh of relief and set the jewelry box and her parents' picture on the table. She rolled her head to one side and then the other. Her stomach gurgled. Hunger pangs gnawed at her. She covered her belly with her hand. Tension drained from her body.

Angela chuckled. "I told you you'd need that granola bar."

At the reminder, her stomach protested even louder. Eleanor laughed. "Apparently so. I better feed myself before I start gnawing on this table." She tore open the package and took a bite. "Mmm... This is really good."

"Food always tastes better after traveling."

Eleanor didn't answer her. She was too busy eating. The bar wasn't going to be enough. "Is there anything more substantial to eat? It feels like I have a pack of ravenous wolves in my stomach."

The other woman grinned. "Yeah, I'm hungry, too, and I already ate breakfast. I'll make us some scrambled eggs while you find that pendant."

Sitting, Eleanor pulled the jewelry box closer. For a moment, she hesitated. Her father had given the unassuming brown jewelry box to her mother for her fiftieth birthday. It didn't look like it would hold anything special. For the most part, it didn't, but it did play a tinny version of the theme from her mother's favorite movie *Somewhere in Time*.

She opened the lid, and a few bars of the theme tinkled through the kitchen. Tears stung Eleanor's eyes, and she blinked. Her mother would make popcorn, and the two of them would sit in the den on a rainy Saturday afternoon and watch the movie, a box of tissues handy. The memory evoked a teary smile. Ah, she missed her mother.

With a last sniffle, she let the memory go, looked down,

and opened the lid. An envelope addressed to her written in her mother's spidery handwriting rested on top. Her hands shook as she reached for it. When would her mom have had time to write this? Did she want to read it?

For several minutes, she stared at the envelope. A bone deep knowing told her this letter would change her life beyond recognition. Her hands trembling, she gently opened the envelope and pulled out the letter. A whisper of her mother's perfume tickled her nose. She blinked back more tears and unfolded the paper.

My Dearest Ellie,

By the time you read this, I will have passed on to meet the Lord. I certainly hadn't intended to leave you alone like this, but God had other plans for me.

I have prayed long about this secret I have carried since your birth. Only as my time grows near do I realize that you must know, that I should have told you long ago. It was wrong of me—of us—to keep it from you, but we feared so many things. We feared you would leave, feared that you would stop loving us, feared things that, now I know in my heart, aren't true.

You see, before I met your father, I fell in love with a man. He was beautiful, intelligent, and kind, and he loved me, but—ah, this is so hard to say. Confessions are not easy. He was not of our world. No, that isn't right. He was from a parallel universe, though he lives on Earth. He claimed he was sent by his people, a far more advanced race than our own, to watch over ours, but he met me and fell in love. The day he asked me to marry him was both joyful and the most terrifying of my life because, before he let me answer, he confessed his true self. He took me through to his homeland to show me. It was beautiful. Beautiful, foreign, frightening, and overwhelming.

I... I was young. I panicked and ran away. When I discovered I was pregnant, I was frantic. Your grandparents would disown me. The father you grew up with, Robert, who was a long time friend, offered to help. He loved me, and I grew to love him with time.

The Whispering House

For years, I feared that your biological father would find me and take you from me. That day, when I saw him in the garden by the tree—

Eleanor looked up from the letter. Her face tingled as the blood drained from it. *Tomani,* her heart cried. Her best friend had been her biological father, and her mother had sent him away. Pain lanced through her. A tear slipped down her nose and dropped onto the paper, staining it. Swiping at her face with her sleeve, she dabbed at the drop and continued to read:

I panicked yet again. If he took you, how would I ever find you? I didn't have his powers. So, God forgive me, but I asked him to go and never return. I took the pendant he gave you and hid it. Why I didn't get rid of it, I don't know. Perhaps God stayed my hand knowing some day I would return it to you.

In time, you forgot about him. In time, I hoped I would. I never did.

Looking back on it, I don't know if what I did was the right thing. Tomani was a good man. But I cannot change the past. I tell you now because you should know and because I believe you share his powers, that some day they may surface.

He told me that if I ever needed him, all I had to do was open my heart to him. I never could bring myself to do it. Robert was my life from the moment we married. Your grandparents never knew. Your aunt does, though.

That explained a lot. Her mother forbidding her to ever play with her jewelry. Her aunt's higher than usual amount of unpleasantness, especially since her parents' deaths, could possibly stem from fear. Maybe it wasn't about control as she'd always believed.

Eleanor sighed and apologized silently to her aunt before returning to the letter.

I hope you can forgive me.
I love you,

Mom

She stared into space for a few minutes, not sure whether to shout in anger, cry in pain, or dance with joy. Her childhood had been a lie. Everything was a lie. The one truth, her one friend, had been banished. Could she forgive her parents? She didn't know. Maybe some day. On the other hand, the discovery that Tomani was her biological dad evoked intense joy. She loved the father she knew, but she had never really connected with him, not like the connection she'd had with Tomani. That she shared his blood, his genes, explained many things.

"Are you okay?"

Angela's voice intruded upon her thoughts. The woman set down a box of tissues. Rather than answer, she handed the letter to the other woman. Angela scanned the letter and looked up at her, eyes full of compassion. She sat in the chair next to her and took Eleanor's hand.

"I thought something like this might have happened."

"How? How could you know and not me?" she asked through her tears. She wanted to scream, but it stuck in the back of her throat.

"I suspected you were more than human. Your powers, they're far beyond what we have. When you told me about the dream and the pendant, I knew you were. This scenario seemed likely. I'm so sorry." She handed Eleanor a tissue and put her arm around her.

Angela's compassion unleashed a dam of sorrow in Eleanor. She cried for her mother, her father, Tomani, and herself. She cried for her lost childhood and for the betrayal. She cried for all the years of feeling out of place, of being misunderstood and lonely. When the tears dried up, Angela stood and walked back to the counter where sandwiches waited.

"Do you know what walking the ley lines is usually like?" She returned to the table and set a sandwich in front of Eleanor.

Eleanor shook her head.

"It's neither as easy nor as quick as what you do. What you do is truly amazing. For the rest of us, a dark, cold tunnel opens up, and depending on how far the destination is from where you are determines how long it takes to get there. It's not unlike driving or flying, although much quicker. It's also exhausting."

Eleanor blew her nose before asking, "Have you ever traveled to the other side of the world using ley lines?"

Angela smiled, a rueful twinkle in her eye. "Once or twice, but it's so taxing that we rarely do it, and the ley lines are used really only in emergencies. Overuse of them creates an imbalance between the parallel universes. Rifts can occur, allowing creatures like the Gehglers to pass through. The past few years, there's been a rise in activity on the lines." She took a bite of her sandwich. "Have you found the pendant yet?"

"No, but it's in the jewelry box. I can feel it in there."

Eleanor set the letter aside and pulled the box toward her. Love and sorrow mingled as she removed each piece of jewelry with care until she reached a silken pouch. A Baroque embroidered flower decorated the pouch. With reverence, she picked it up. It pulsed in her hand, sending tingles up her arm. She unzipped it and lifted the delicate silver chain. The pendant, with an opalescent unicorn carved in it, dangled from the chain. A rainbow spiraled from the bottom of its horn to the tip.

"I've never seen one of these. May I touch it?" Angela reached out before Eleanor could respond. Sparks flew, and she snatched it back with a startled yelp.

"Apparently not," Eleanor said. She slipped the necklace on then touched the pendant. In a trance, she gazed unseeing at the table. The heady knowledge of another world and of her powers filled her. Words spilled from her lips. "This pendant is called a *fesuhn*. It's a powerful amulet designed to protect one person for their lifetime. Each *fesuhn* is calibrated to the DNA of its wearer. It will defend itself and the wearer should someone try to steal it or take it from its owner without permission."

She blinked and stared at the pendant. Tiny specks of golden light sparkled in the body of the unicorn. Part of her wanted to run away and deny everything, but another part leapt with joy. She sat straighter. This was her heritage, but she had to be careful. The power could be used for good or could corrupt.

"How did your mother get it from you then?" Angela asked.

"She asked. While I wasn't completely willing, she was my mother, so I gave it to her of my own choice."

In her mind, a faint scream of anger echoed, and she shivered. The Gehglers were still out there, searching. They wouldn't find her, but she sensed things were about to get ugly.

Chapter Twenty

For the next couple of days, her days consisted of eating, training, and sleeping. Each day, she focused on learning to control her abilities. Each night, exhausted, she fell into a dreamless sleep. The pendant had remained silent, and only occasionally did knowledge come to her as it did that first day at the kitchen table.

On the third morning, Eleanor woke early. Lying in bed, she stared at the ceiling. It was time to move. The Gehglers were closing in on their location. She sensed it. At some point, she would have to face them, but she wasn't ready. Today, they needed to wash their clothes, pack, and leave.

At breakfast, she told Angela and Heather.

Angela sighed. "I've sensed it as well."

"Perhaps you need to go some place not owned by a keeper," Heather said. "Esme knows the keepers."

Angela filled her in on the latest news and said, "But we don't want to endanger someone. Eleanor almost succumbed to their mind control when we retrieved the *fesuhn*. They have her officer friend. It may be too late to help him, and that may be the way they've tracked us down."

Dizziness hit Eleanor as she realized the implications. She hadn't considered what this could mean for Rodney. They'd taken control of him, she understood that, but she hadn't thought beyond it. So much had occurred in such a short time, and she was just trying to survive.

"What do you mean it may be too late to help Rodney?"

Heather reached out and squeezed her hand. "Unless we can release him soon, he may not come out of this."

Her eyes widened. "What? No."

Angela nodded. "Sadly, she's right. There might be some hope, but I wouldn't count on it."

"Then what happens to him?" Eleanor asked.

"He'll eventually go mad. For some, it happens sooner than others."

"And then?"

Angela paused.

"Angela, what happens after that?"

"Well, if he's mad, he's no use to them. He has to be functioning at a certain level for him to have any value."

"And?"

Angela and Heather exchanged a look but neither said anything.

"Well?"

"You know those gruesome murders where the people are half eaten?"

Her stomach dropped. "They don't—"

"The Gehglers will kill him and eat him."

Frantic, Eleanor stood. "I have to save him." She looked around for a weapon.

Angela grabbed her arm. "Weapons won't work with them. Not the kind you're thinking of. The best thing you can do is to develop your powers and help us close the ley lines."

Sadness and guilt weighed on her. Her shoulders slumped. Rodney had been trying to help, and she'd repaid him with this.

"Hey." Angela's voice broke into her thoughts. "You can't blame yourself for this."

"But if I—"

"No," she said. "This is not your fault. You didn't know. This could've happened at any time. The next person who moved in there could've ended up like Rodney. He could've gone to answer a call there and had the same thing happen with, or without, you. Besides, guilt won't help you."

"She's right." Heather stood and carried her dishes to the sink. She turned and leaned against the counter. "Had you been there, they would've gotten you. There was nothing you could do. As it stands, there's still a possibility of saving him."

Hope flared in Eleanor. "There is?"

"It's slim, but, yes."

Angela glared at the other woman. "It's *very* slim."

"But it's still there."

"How much time do we have?" Eleanor asked.

"It's hard to say," Angela said. "It depends on a lot of things. A few more days, a week max."

Eleanor deflated again and then raised her head. Determined, she wouldn't be defeated. As long as he wasn't dead, she would still hope. Pushing her chair back from the table, she stood and grabbed her plate.

Heather held out her hand. "Let me take care of that. Gather your things and prepare to leave."

"Thanks. I want to call Michael. If Lily has been struggling, I'm sure he has, too. I need to know."

As she left the kitchen, Angela's voice drifted into the hallway.

"You shouldn't have told her she could help him. It's too late for him. Once they take over a person, they're never free."

"What would you suggest? You saw her. We need her focused and moving forward right now. Better false hope than no hope."

She braced herself against the wall to stop herself from collapsing. Resting her head against the cool wall, she gasped in deep breaths before straightening her spine. Angela had said she'd never seen anyone with her powers before. Maybe they were wrong. They had to be wrong.

* * * *

In her bedroom, she unplugged her cellphone and stared at her phone. Once again, she'd forgotten to get his phone number. After what she'd heard in the hallway, going back into the kitchen didn't appeal. She sat on the bed and put her head in her hands. If only Michael were there. He'd put his arms around her, and she'd forget for a moment. She imagined what it would be like to have him standing next to her, his arms around her. His words from what seemed like years ago echoed in her head. *All you have to do is call.* She hadn't needed a phone in the past, but was it safe to call him that way? Would it attract the Gehglers to them? Her pendant had prevented them from tracking their travel from her house. Could it work with this, too?

The yearning inside her intensified. Her heart whispered his name. Suddenly, the air shimmered in front of her, and he appeared. Dark circles haunted his eyes. His cheekbones stood out in stark relief, stubble covered his cheeks and chin. It looked as if he hadn't slept for days.

Not quite believing it was true, she reached out and said, "Michael?" Her hand encountered a solid chest. It radiated heat, and she struggled not to lean into him.

"Eleanor," he breathed. "Why did you call me?" Concern and hunger shimmered in his eyes.

"I... I had to see you." She hated the neediness in her voice, hated the neediness period, but she couldn't hide or deny it. Too much had occurred. It was all she could do not to touch him again. Instead, she asked, "How are you?"

"It's been rough at home, Eleanor, but we've finally got it under control...I hope." Tension emanated from him. "I shouldn't be here."

She sighed. "I'm sorry."

He stared at her for a moment in silence before saying, "It's all right. I've been wanting to see you, to see if you're okay. You can't blame yourself for what's happening."

"But if I hadn't—"

"If it hadn't been you, it would've been someone else. I'm sure Angela has told you the activity has increased over the past couple of years."

She nodded. "Yes, she did."

"We've never seen it like this, I admit. They've killed a few head of our cattle, but I've managed to stop that by keeping the herd in a pen close to the house. As of now, our house has escaped unscathed, unlike Lily's."

"Oh, Michael..."

"It's okay. We're doing okay." He sounded tired.

"They have Rodney, you know."

"I heard. I'm sorry."

She looked down at her hands gripped tightly in front of her. "There's nothing you could've done. None of us were there."

Why didn't he touch her? Why didn't she touch him? They didn't have time for this. She needed to send him back. She should be packing, but she couldn't bring herself to do it. Oh, how she wanted him.

"Eleanor."

He said her name right before he cupped her cheek.

She leaned into it and closed her eyes. Her eyes stung, tears sprang up. They slipped out of her eyes and splashed on his hand.

"Sweetheart, it's going to be all right."

Something inside of her melted. Even though he'd spent the past few days fighting the Gehglers, he still thought of her. She choked on a sob, and his arms encircled her. Snuggling into his chest, she clung to him, but she wanted more, more than this platonic hug. She needed to chase the pain away, to feel connected to another human being, to feel that life wasn't completely out of control.

Raising her head, she looked into his face. The muscles in his jaw clenched. Passion flared in his eyes. At the stark look of desire on his face, heat coursed through her. Unable to help herself, she drew his face down to hers and kissed him. He groaned and crushed her to him, sliding his hands down to cup her ass and pull her tight against him. His erection pressed against her, and she moaned.

God, she needed this.

A loud knock sounded on the door.

"Eleanor," Angela said from the other side. "Are you okay?"

They froze, and Eleanor swallowed a nervous giggle.

"Uh, yeah, I'm fine."

"Okay. I thought I heard someone else's voice. Are you sure you're okay?"

Eleanor's gaze darted up to Michael's. Should they tell her? He shook his head. Smoldering passion glinted in his tawny gaze, turning it molten. She shivered, her nipples pebbled, and goose bumps shimmied down her entire body. His arms tightened around her.

Breathless, she struggled to answer with a normal voice. "Yes, yes, I'm fine."

"All right, if you say so. We need to leave soon."

"I know. I'll be ready. I'll meet you in the kitchen."

"Okay."

Michael raised an eyebrow at her, a question lurking in his eyes.

She mouthed, "I'll tell you when she leaves."

He nodded.

A few minutes later, she opened the door and looked out. The hallway was empty. Relief and shame flooded her. She'd never done anything like this in her life. Even if she had no reason to feel shamed, it squelched any desire that lingered within her.

She shut the door with an inaudible click and turned back to Michael. Eyes full of passion burned a path of heat down her body. She shivered. Despite the shame, desire ignited again, and the urge to touch him increased. Leaning against the door, she fought to control her cravings. They didn't have time for this. What was she thinking bringing him here? Angela would return any minute, the Gehglers with Rodney were on their way, and she still had to pack.

With a deep breath, she pushed away from the door. "Okay. I shouldn't have brought you here. I'm sorry. There isn't time for this, and I wasn't thinking."

"Why did you bring me here?"

"I... I honestly don't know. Everything that's happened just seemed too much. I needed... I needed some human contact..."

A rueful smile teased the corners of his mouth. "Human contact? I had hoped to be more than that."

"You are. I mean..." She crossed to him and touched his arm then jerked her hand away quickly as sparks danced between them. "I don't know what I mean. At the moment, you're someone I trust, someone I am so attracted to I do things I shouldn't, someone I—"

He captured her mouth with his in a kiss that left her weak-kneed and gasping. When the kiss ended, she clung to him and dropped her head to his chest. Wrapping her arms around him, she forgot what she was going to say, her mind in a jumble.

With a finger under her chin, he tilted her head back, and their gazes met. Passion flickered in his eyes. Every cell in her body wanted to kiss him again, to undress him, and explore every inch of his hard body, but she couldn't.

"I get it," he said. "You're overwhelmed and needed comfort."

She nodded. "Yes. It's been hard. The things that have happened, Michael..."

The horror of the past couple of days threatened to trap her in a mental net she might not escape. To break it, she leaned into him. His arms tightened around her.

"What am I going to do, Michael?" she whispered.

"I'm here. You'll be fine."

"What if I'm not?"

He moved her away from him, his face stern. "You'll be fine. We'll keep you safe, and this will pass."

"What if you can't and it doesn't?"

"We will." He stepped back. "Now, you need to pack, but first you need to send me back."

"You aren't surprised that I brought you here?"

He shook his head and smiled. "From the moment I saw you, Eleanor, I knew."

"What did you know?"

"You have Itari blood in you," he said.

"Itari blood?" What, or who, were Itari?

"They're an advanced humanoid race from a parallel dimension. Hasn't anyone told you yet?"

She shook her head and touched her pendant. It pulsed in her hand. No one had told her the name of the race, not even her mother. "I know my father is, yes, but I didn't know their name." Cocking her head to the side, she studied him. "You are, too, aren't you?"

A rich chuckle warmed the air between them. "I am."

"So, that's how your family knew."

"Yes."

"Then you can travel like me?"

He nodded.

"Then why do you need me to send you back? Don't all Itari have these powers?"

"They do, but, in this instance, we don't want to cause too many ripples in ley lines. It will make it easier for the Gehglers to find you." The light mood disappeared with his statement, and reality set in.

She shrunk back at the mention of the creatures who hunted her. "Oh."

"Now, can I go back?" he asked. "I've been away too long as it is." Nodding, she opened the portal to his house. He dropped a quick kiss on her lips and stepped through.

Turning back to her, he said, "You can always call on me, Eleanor. Any time, any where, I will come." Something other than passion glinted his eyes.

Her heart leapt. Was it possible? No, it couldn't be. Before she could ask him anything more, the air shimmered, and he disappeared. Frustration filled her. Once again, she'd forgotten to ask him for his phone number.

Chapter Twenty-One

Fifteen minutes later, they were packed and had moved to another keeper's house. When Angela tried to start their training sessions again, Eleanor struggled to focus. The memory of Michael's kiss and the last look he'd given her destroyed her concentration. Part of her wanted to call him to her and finish what they'd started. Another part warned against it. With everything that was going on, she couldn't afford the distraction. But, of course, she was distracted. After a half hour of training, they gave up and took a break for the rest of the day.

While Eleanor and Angela were packing, Heather had called a couple of keepers before she found one home. The news of the Gehglers and Esme had traveled the circuit. Every keeper was ready to offer a safe place for the two women. Joe just happened to be home. This time, they'd landed in Longwood, Florida, a suburb of Orlando.

Eleanor wiped the sweat from her forehead and stared out the window on the screened in porch at the cypress trees and staghorn ferns. If her mind hadn't been focused on Michael, the peace of her surroundings might've wrapped her in its silken binds and soothed her.

The *fesuhn* tingled against the skin between her breasts. She pulled it out from under her shirt and fingered it. Warmth emanated from it. Undoing the latch, she studied the glowing pendant. Opalescent sparks swirled across the unicorn's body, giving the illusion that it was alive. The colors on the horn gyrated. Everything disappeared but the pendant. A beautiful song echoed along her nerve endings, and memories of her father spilled forth. Her childish laughter rang in her ears. His kind face and piercing silver gray eyes... Eyes just like her own. She'd inherited her mother's brown hair, but her father had gifted her with his beautiful eyes—her favorite feature.

"Oh, Tomani," she whispered, her heart full of love for the man who'd honored her mother's wishes even though it meant leaving his beloved child. And she was beloved to him.

"Eleanor?"

Eleanor jerked, looking around at the sound of a man's voice. Who said that? Angela was napping, and Joe, their host, had left until evening. Her gaze lit upon a man standing on the other side of the screen. Although many years had passed, the eyes, the voice, the silvery blond hair, could only belong to one person.

"Tomani?" she said in disbelief.

He smiled and nodded.

"It's really you?"

He laughed and nodded again.

"I'm not imagining you?"

"No, you're not." His smile lit his eyes, and they shone like polished silver. "It's good to speak to you, Leeli."

Her breath caught at his use of her pet name. It was one thing to hear it in her mind, but to hear him actually say it aloud after all these years? It felt unreal.

"Would you like to go for a walk with me?" he asked.

"I'd love to," she said, "but I need to let my friend Angela know so she doesn't worry. Would you like to wait inside while I tell her?"

"No, thank you. The trees are humming. I'm enjoying their music. Do you remember when we used to sit outside and listen to the trees in your yard hum?"

The question evoked a memory of lying under the trees in her backyard with Tomani by her side and listening to nature sing. Every living thing had a voice, even the rocks. She smiled.

"I do. How did I forget about that?"

"Go tell your friend you're going for a walk. We can talk about it in the trees."

"Okay." What did he mean they'd talk about it?

She turned and went to find Angela. A few minutes later, she joined Tomani outside.

"Come," he said and started down a path.

She walked beside him in silence. Dappled sunlight created patterns on the ground. The wind soughed through the branches of the tall cypress trees. Eleanor sighed. Tension trickled out of her. Her shoulders relaxed, and the muscles in her neck released.

"Better?" he asked.

"Yes." She glanced at him. "How did you know?"

He stopped and faced her. Compassion radiated from him. "It's to be expected. Leeli, your abilities couldn't stay suppressed any longer. Now that they have surfaced again, it will take time to adjust."

"What do you mean? I didn't suppress anything. I never had these abilities." Anger surged through her. How could he say that to her?

"Yes, you did. You did it to gain acceptance from your mother and father."

She snorted. There had never been acceptance. They always pushed her to be something she wasn't. Nothing she did satisfied them.

He touched her arm. She turned her face away. She couldn't bear to look at him, to see the pity in his face.

"Leeli, they loved you, but they didn't know how to handle you. Like every child, you wanted to please your parents. They couldn't accept you as you were. They didn't know how. That didn't mean they didn't love you."

"That makes no sense. How can you love someone and yet not accept them for who they are?"

"Did you love your mother?"

"Of course. She was my mother."

"And yet you haven't accepted her for who she was."

"That's not..." She couldn't finish her sentence. He was right. She couldn't accept her mother's behavior toward her or her decision to send Tomani away. Disgusted and angry, she strode over to the edge of the path and leaned her head against a tree.

"Your mother did the best she could. Just like you did. Just like your father and aunt did."

An inarticulate sound escaped her. Emotions she'd tamped down for years welled up and threatened to overcome her. She struggled to shove them back down, but the walls that had kept them contained shuddered and crumbled. Anger, fear, frustration, and helplessness rushed over her. She sunk down until she crouched at the base of the tree, her arms wrapped tight around her knees.

"Forgive them. It's the only way."

"How?" She turned a tear-streaked face to him. "How do I forgive them when I can't forgive myself? And then you left me with them. Alone. Every time I used any of my abilities, I was punished. I only wanted them to be proud of me, of what I could do."

"They were afraid. What if someone else saw? What if someone took you away? What if you disappeared and never returned?"

He walked over and knelt next to her. Gently, he drew her into his arms and held her. She relaxed against him. This was the Tomani she remembered. This was her father. The man her mother had married, the man who'd raised her deserved a place in her heart, but, this man, he understood and loved her for who she was. He would never try to change her.

In a small voice, she said, "Papa, I love you."

Tomani gasped. His arms tightened around her. When he spoke, his voice shook. "*Mir shoben, Io ten zajen.*"

How long they remained that way, Eleanor didn't know. Her legs tingled, and she moved out of his embrace to sit on the ground, stretching her legs out in front of her. He settled next to her, holding her hand.

"Listen. Do you hear it? Can you hear nature sing?"

Eleanor fought her way through the tumult inside of her and strained to hear the music she remembered from her childhood.

"You're trying too hard, *mishka*. You can't hear it with your ears. You must listen with your heart. Open your heart," Tomani said. "If you let them, they will sing to you."

At first, she heard only the beating of her heart, the sound of the animals rustling in the bush, the wind soughing in the trees high above. But the longer she sat listening with no expectations, a soft melody rose around her. Behind her, the tree hummed. Its energy wrapped her in a soothing cocoon. The surrounding trees hummed in unison. The melody undulated through the woods. The warble of a bird sang in counterpoint. A frog croaked in the distance. Every sound had its place within nature's symphony. She sensed that, if one song went missing, it all fell apart.

Reverence filled her at the gift she was being given.

"You hear it," he whispered.

It wasn't a question. She nodded, loath to break the spell. For several minutes, they listened to nature sing.

"Eleanor, we need to talk. This isn't why I asked you to walk with me."

He'd never called her by her real name.

"It's the Gehglers, isn't it?"

He nodded. "I won't be able to help you with this. While you are part Itari, I'm not allowed to interfere with the happenings of this universe. I can only observe."

"And if they get me?"

"They won't."

"I don't want to spend my life running. I don't want others in danger because of me."

"The answers will come. It'll just take time." He stood and offered her a hand. "It's time to return to the house."

"Wait! What about Rodney?"

"I'm sorry."

"What do you mean, 'I'm sorry?' I won't give up on him."

"Leeli—"

"No, I refuse to let them have him."

"There's nothing you can do."

"Angela said that if I got to him soon enough, we might be able to get him back."

He sighed, his eyes full of compassion. "When the Gehglers take over another being, things change within them. They're never the same. The Rodney you met won't be the same Rodney after. Even if you can 'save' him, he will be damaged."

"So, what, I'm just supposed to let them eat him?" She stopped walking and glared at him. "How is that okay?"

"Even if something could be done, it's—"

"You're saying you can do something for him? That it's possible?" Hope burgeoned in her chest.

He started back toward the house again, avoiding her gaze. "It wouldn't matter if I could or not. I can't interfere. It's forbidden."

"But—"

"No, you don't understand." He stopped. The look in his

eyes spoke of deep sorrow. "Were I to interfere, I would be banished from ever visiting here again. I would never see you again. And, you, you wouldn't be able to visit Itar. I can't lose you after all of this time."

A crushing weight settled upon her. To never see him again... There had to be a way around this. She couldn't let Rodney die without at least trying to save him. "Could I do it if I knew how? Could you instruct me?"

"I don't know. I'll have to ask. There are reasons for not interfering. It isn't just a random law."

"But the Gehglers do it," she protested.

He ran his hand through his hair. "The Gehglers don't care about how their actions alter other parallel universes or the races that live in them. The Itari do. To continue an upward evolution, which is our goal, we must be aware of how our actions affect every living creature, no matter the degree of sentience, in every universe we visit. In practice, that means everything. However, I'll let them know what's happening here. They may allow me to instruct you, but it will most likely come with a price."

If she could save him, she would do it. "I'm willing to pay it."

Tomani shook his head. "Because you're not familiar with our race, I won't accept that promise yet. Until you know the price, don't say anything."

They walked in silence for the rest of the way to Joe's house. Excitement, coupled with relief, at the prospect of saving Rodney built inside her. She couldn't wait to tell Angela.

When they reached the property boundary, he halted. "You must tell no one until we've gained permission. Even then, it can only be a few," he said, as if reading her mind.

"What? Why?"

"If it gets out that we've done this, we'll be bombarded with requests. The path of evolution for any race, but our own, cannot be accelerated or changed... at least, not by us. It's a sacred vow every Itari has taken."

"How do you know?" she asked.

He raised his eyebrows at her. As serious as this situation was, she couldn't contain the chuckle that escaped her.

Humans would grab these powers and manipulate them. One country would use them to control all the others. Until they could end the wars, the violence, the abuse, the hatred, the prejudice, Itari-like powers would lead to a downward spiral. Heck, without them, some days it seemed like they were already on their way.

"I must leave now. I've been here longer than I meant to stay."

Her heart dropped. "When will I see you again?"

"Soon. If you're going to save Rodney, you must act within the week. Whether you'll be ready or not, I don't know."

"What if I fail? What if they get me when I try to save him?"

His fierce stare pierced her. "That won't happen."

"You can't know."

He clenched his hand. "I won't let it happen."

"But you can't interfere..."

His head dropped to his chest, and a look of agony crossed his face. "I know," he whispered, "but I'll die before I let harm come to you."

She caressed his face and lifted it so she could look into his eyes. "I won't die, Papa."

He pulled her to him in a tight hug and kissed the top of her head. Love encircled her, and a contented smile tugged at her lips.

Stepping back, he held her by the shoulders and regarded her with a serious expression. "Promise me you'll forgive your mother, your adopted father, and yourself. When you do, you'll be able to heal the wound inside of you, and the anger you've felt all of your life will melt away. Until then, we won't be able to go forward."

"I—I'll try."

"You can't try. You must, or your friend will be lost."

A pit formed in her stomach. How could she forgive them when she struggled to forgive herself? It might never happen. Rodney would die if she didn't find a way to do it. Could she? Would she? God, she hoped so, or she'd never forgive herself.

Chapter Twenty-Two

After Tomani left, Eleanor returned to the spot where he'd found her. The tranquility she'd found sitting under the tree and talking with him had vanished. In its place, fear, anger, and despair raged. How did one forgive oneself? She'd been trying for years and never succeeded. Now, she either did it or let those nasty, little creatures take an innocent man. Even if she forgave herself and her parents, that didn't mean Tomani would help her. The powers that be in Itar may deny him.

Why was life always so complicated? Why couldn't she float along in a happy cloud like her friend Jennifer did? No, she had to be half advanced humanoid-half human hunted by a scary humanoid from a parallel universe. Nothing could ever go smoothly. That would be against all the laws in the universe. No, it had to be "let's torment Eleanor" every day of the week.

"Did you have a good walk?" Angela's voice intruded on her roiling thoughts. She sat next to Eleanor on the porch swing.

With a sigh, she nodded. "Yes." She turned to her mentor. "Angela, have you ever wondered why you? Why you were chosen for what you do?"

She shrugged. "No, not really. I was raised to be a keeper. I never questioned it."

"Must be nice," Eleanor muttered.

"No, it wasn't. Not all of the time. Sometimes, it was lonely. I couldn't tell my friends. Try that while going through puberty and high school." Angela chuckled. "I was as full of angst as the next person, but I never questioned that I was going to be a keeper. The importance of the job, the honor of being 'chosen', that eventually overcame everything else."

"You were never angry?"

She shrugged. "Oh, during high school, I had my moments, but the anger faded. It was too cool. No, I couldn't take any friends through the ley lines, but no one else could do what I did. That was cool."

"But your parents supported you. They didn't punish you for your abilities."

Angela turned to face Eleanor. Grabbing her hand, she squeezed it. "Oh, Eleanor, I'm sorry. Your situation is different than mine. You have a lot to absorb. So much has happened in such a short time. It must be hard. I would be angry, too."

She looked down at Angela's hand covering her tightly clasped ones. "Except I don't have time to be angry at anyone. I have to find a way to forgive my parents, myself, so that I can move on and save Rodney."

"About that—"

"I heard you and Heather talking. Even if it's a slim chance, I have to try. But in order to even get to that point, I have to forgive." Her eyes swimming with tears, she looked up at Angela. "I've been carrying this anger at them for years. I didn't know it until all of this happened." She raised her arms in disgust and stared out at the trees. "How do you not know something like that?"

"I—"

"Seriously, how do you not know?" She snorted in derision.

"You bury it because, if you don't, it kills everything."

"Well, now, if I don't deal with it, it will result in the death of an innocent man. So what do I do?" Despair threatened to take her down once again.

Angela leaned forward, forcing Eleanor to look at her. "Don't. It wasn't your fault."

"If I—"

"It. Wasn't. Your. Fault. You can't take responsibility for something you couldn't control. Life is full of those moments. You'll bury yourself with regret and stagnate because you'll be mired in the quicksand of self-flagellation. It helps no one."

"But—"

"No buts. If you want to forgive, you have to recognize this first," Angela said.

"I—"

"You can't control everything, Eleanor. As I'm sure you

know, you can—"

"Only control how I respond." How many self-help gurus had she heard say *that*? She snorted. If she had a nickel... They were right, though. Knowing and practicing were two different things. She sighed. "So, what do you suggest?"

"I suggest you ask yourself what would help you forgive yourself and your parents."

"And if I don't get an answer?"

"Then Rodney is dead."

* * * *

Several hours later, Eleanor lay on the bed in her room staring at the ceiling. So far, she'd found a lion, an angel, a pyramid, and an odd looking face in the stucco ceiling, but still no answers, still no progress on forgiving herself. She'd also memorized the landscape on the wall and identified at least ten different hues of ocean blue. It was a peaceful painting and made her wish to be there. Of course, anywhere but where she currently was would work.

"Just forgive yourself," they said. "Your inner self will tell you what to do." Because her inner self *always* talked to her. Sure, it did. Just like cherries were blue and the sun orbited the Earth.

"Just forgive yourself." Because that was so easy. And no advice on how to do it. Typical, she was on her own. If she'd known that moving to the countryside of Fresno would start this whole ordeal, she would've listened to her aunt and stayed in San Jose. The freedom she'd craved, the new life that had looked so appealing, even after that first run in with the Gehglers, had lost its luster. Healing from her parents' deaths now included forgiving them, and herself, to prevent the death of an innocent man. All because of her stupid desire to be "free" of her family.

And beating herself up wasn't going to help. She had to figure out this forgiveness thing and save Rodney.

One thing at a time, Ellie, she told herself. *First, forgiveness.*

How did one forgive anyone? Where did one start?

"Bah!" Frustrated, she rose and crossed to the window.

Stars twinkled high above framed by the branches of the giant cypress trees. If only their serenity could spread through her.

Grabbing a sweater, she left the room for the backyard. The evening air nipped at her arms. She slipped the sweater over her head and stared up at the sky. An owl hooted in the distance, but, otherwise, it was silent. Did the world sing at night?

Listen with your heart, Tomani's voice whispered.

Perhaps if she touched a tree, it would work. But what good would this do? The singing wouldn't bring answers. No, but it had brought her peace. And, maybe from a peaceful place, the answers would come. It was worth a shot. Staring at the ceiling certainly hadn't worked.

Crossing to a giant cypress growing along the edge of the yard, she touched the trunk of the tree. The bark felt cold beneath her hand. The forest remained silent. She leaned into the tree. Nothing.

She released a frustrated breath. What was she doing? This was useless.

She pushed away from the tree. Pain lanced her heart. Rodney would die. She couldn't do it. She didn't know how, and no one would give her guidance. If she failed with Rodney, what would happen to her? Would the Gehglers get her, too? Anything was possible if she didn't find the key to forgiveness.

A tear trickled down her cheek. She swiped at it. God, she cried all the time now. She hated it, hated everything about her life now.

Even Michael and your father?

She jerked and looked around the yard. Nothing stirred, not even the wind. Where had that voice come from?

And then, as if someone flipped a switch, music poured through the backyard. Intricate harmonies swirled around her, caressing her. Joyous melodies tugged at her, inviting her to dance.

Shaking her head, she crossed her arms. How could she dance when her world was caving in?

The melodies softened to a plaintive, haunting tune. They wrapped around her heart, penetrated her soul, and filled the empty, aching spots. As her despair loosened, the music lightened. It flowed like a burbling creek. Her spirits rose with the crescendoing music until she could stand still no more. With joy propelling her on, she leapt and pirouetted along the edge of the lawn under the protection of the trees. The music reached an apex, and its tempo slowed, the urgency of moments before becoming a faint echo. Her feet slowed until she swayed to the soft lullaby. Peace replaced the despondency, and knowledge of what her next step had to be filled her.

"Thank you," she whispered.

A breeze lifted the edge of her hair. Goose bumps shimmied across her skin. She smiled.

Chapter Twenty-Three

Back in her room, Eleanor gathered her belongings. Although they were safe at Joe's house, she had to leave.

"What are you doing?" Angela asked when she walked into the room.

Eleanor paused to look up before placing the last shirt in the suitcase. Next to it, she set her toiletries bag. "I have to go visit my aunt."

"What? Why? You can't—"

"I have to. If this is going to end, if I'm going to save Rodney and myself, I have to talk to my aunt."

"Eleanor—"

She put up her hand to silence her. "No, this has to be done."

"You'll put them in danger," Angela protested.

"They'll be fine. The Gehglers won't even know I'm there." Closing the suitcase, she zipped it up and set it on the floor. "Are you coming? Or do you want to stay?"

Stunned, the keeper said, "I'll go pack. It shouldn't take me long."

"Is Joe around?" Eleanor asked.

"No."

"Then I'll leave a note thanking him. I hope he doesn't mind."

Angela shrugged. "He's aware of the situation. I doubt he'll mind." She turned and crossed the room. Stopping at the door, she looked at Eleanor. "Do you think we'll be back?"

"I don't know. We'll see."

* * * *

Sometime later, they stood on the sidewalk in the front of her aunt's house, suitcases in hand. The pale blue, ranch house looked inviting in the waning daylight. Light shone from the paned windows. A concrete walkway split the lawn in two. Waist-high shrubs edged the lawn on the left side, separating her yard from the neighbor's. Her aunt and uncle's silver Toyota Corolla sat in the driveway on the right.

Eleanor shivered, rubbing her arms against the chill of the San Jose winter evening. For a moment, she hesitated. Was she doing the right thing? She could walk away before her aunt saw them. No one would know. No, she had to do this. Everything hinged on this happening.

With a deep breath, she stepped toward the house and strode up the walkway, rolling her suitcase behind her. Angela followed her.

"How long do you think we'll stay?" Angela asked when they stopped at the door.

"I don't know. We may not stay at all." She looked at her friend.

"Why?"

"You'll know when you meet my aunt. I love her, but..." How did one explain the type of relationship she had with her aunt? "Maybe I'll tell you why some other time. Right now, I'd just like to get this over."

"That bad?"

She shrugged and gave her a half smile. "Maybe. We'll talk about it some other time."

She faced the door and rang the doorbell.

A few minutes passed before they heard someone approach the door and the lock disengage. The door opened to her aunt's stunned face. A wrinkled hand pressed against her chest as if she were startled at the sight of them. The expression faded quickly and was replaced by one of distrust.

"So, you finally decided to show up?" Her brown eyes hardened when they rested on the suitcases and Angela. The corners of her mouth turned down. "Do you plan to stay?"

"No. My friend, Angela, and I are just passing through." Her aunt just nodded. "We need to talk. May we come in?"

"I..." She glanced to Angela. Her salt and pepper hair framed her angular face and long nose, emphasizing her scrutiny. "I suppose. I was about to eat dinner, but it can wait." Her aunt turned away and walked further into the house.

Accustomed to her aunt's cold welcome, Eleanor looked at Angela and bit her lip to stop her laughter. Her aunt always had that effect on people. Exposure didn't improve it either.

"Wow," Angela mouthed, her eyes wide.

Eleanor shrugged. As long as she could remember, her aunt had always been this way. How her uncle had married her and stayed with her all of these years puzzled Eleanor, but he had. Perhaps he saw a side of her that no one else did. Even their children spent as little time with her as possible, although they weren't much better.

The interior of the house hadn't changed since Eleanor had last visited. Actually, it hadn't changed since the late-eighties when her aunt paid some interior designer to decorate it. The Southwestern decor belonged in Sedona, not Willow Glen, San Jose. They pulled their suitcases into the living room. A blanket with a Native American design covered the back of the brown leather couch.

"Hi, Uncle Nate," she said.

Her uncle looked up from his dinner at the dining room table. He waved to her, his expression uninterested and preoccupied. A newspaper lay open on the table in front of him.

Her aunt threw her a sour look. "Why don't you take a seat?" She situated herself in a wing chair across from the couch.

A look passed between Eleanor and Angela before they sat down.

"I see you're none the worse for wear," her aunt said. "I did call the police and told them the missing person's report had been a mistake. They kept me on hold for what seemed like hours, but I got it done."

"Thank you, Aunt Shirley. I appreciate it."

"Why couldn't you call them yourself?" her aunt demanded. The edge in her voice suggested she thought her niece was in trouble and in hiding.

"I was in a hurry, and I told you Officer Tyler has been stalking me. I didn't want him to find out where I was," Eleanor said.

Aunt Shirley waved her hand, dismissing her niece's excuse. "So, why did you come here?"

"We need to talk."

Her aunt snorted. "You've said that already. Get to the

point, girl, my dinner's getting cold."

Without saying another word, Eleanor pulled the *fesuhn* out from under her shirt.

The color drained from her aunt's face, and fear glinted in her eyes. Her hand shook as she reached for her glasses that lay on the end table next to her chair. "Where did you get that...that thing?"

"I found it in Mom's jewelry box with a letter." Eleanor fingered the pendant. It grew warm in her hands.

The older woman gasped and cowered. "You aren't going to harm me, are you?"

"What? No. Why would you think that?"

At Eleanor's response, her aunt leaned forward and said, "Because you're the spawn of Satan. I urged your mother to get an abortion when she told me she was pregnant with that demon's seed, but she refused. Now, you come to my door wearing that amulet intent on doing evil."

Eleanor's eyes widened. Even for her aunt, the attack was vicious. "I am not the spawn of Satan."

Aunt Shirley sneered at her. "I saw your demon father, who looked like an angel, spirit my sister away that day. I was there. They didn't see me, but I saw them. They just disappeared. Your mother never did have any sense when she was young. I thought maybe if you spent enough time in church, you could overcome your blood. Well, apparently, I was wrong. Do you know that I told our parents about your father, but they didn't believe me?" Her eyes narrowed. "Your mother always was the favorite. She could never do wrong. Even when she stole my beau so that she wouldn't shame the family with a bastard."

"Shirley," her uncle said, interrupting the tirade, "that's enough."

The woman clamped her lips together and scowled.

Compassion flooded Eleanor. No wonder her aunt was so sour. She reached out to touch her and apologize, but her aunt recoiled as if Eleanor had an infectious disease.

"Don't touch me. Get out. If you're going to wear that thing around your neck, you're no longer welcome here."

"Shirley." Her uncle's deep voice held a warning in it.

Her aunt faced her husband. "I won't tolerate it, Nathan.

I've put up with her for 35 years. I've done my best. Nothing more can be done." Turning back to the two women on the couch, she said, "I bet you were lying about Officer Rodney. I bet you committed some crime and fled, but you had ensorcelled him somehow. Rather than report you, he filed a missing person's report."

"What? No. Why would I lie?"

"Because you're evil. Evil always lies."

Her plans were spinning away from her. Any hope she had of saving Rodney was dwindling fast. "I was hoping you'd go with me to the cemetery to visit Mom and Dad," she said, trying one last time to reach her aunt.

"Now? What? Do you plan to dig her up and eat her bones?"

"Never mind, Aunt Shirley. We'll get there on our own."

"Demon travel. Just like your father." She stood and marched to the door, yanking it open. "Leave and don't come back."

Angela followed her to the door. They stepped out into the cold winter night. Eleanor's shoulders drooped.

Now what was she to do?

Chapter Twenty-Four

The two women stood on the sidewalk. Neither said a word. Eleanor shivered. She should've seen this coming. Never an easy person at the best of times, her aunt Shirley's behavior exceeded anything Eleanor had ever seen from her before. Her aunt's confession explained a lot. It made it easier to forgive a bitter, old woman, but it stung that she viewed her own niece as demon spawn, despite all of the years in her company. Her aunt deserved her pity, not anger.

"Your aunt is..." Angela paused.

"Bitter and jealous." She looked at her friend. "I never knew. Family secrets can be pretty ugly. I'd rather not have known. I'm sorry you experienced it."

"So, what do you suggest now?" she asked.

"I don't know."

"Maybe we should go to your parents' grave."

"I suppose."

"What do you have to lose? And why did you need your aunt to go with you?"

Eleanor looked up at the sky. A sickle moon shone stark against the ebony backdrop of space. One or two stars twinkled, but the rest couldn't compete with the lights of the city. She missed her small house on the outskirts of Fresno. Why couldn't it have continued the way it had started?

Turning to Angela, she said, "She needed to be there for my plan to work. I planned on forgiving them all together."

"Can you forgive her now? Now that you know everything?"

She nodded. "Yes. I'm no longer angry with her. I pity her, but I'm not angry. My uncle is a saint to stay with her."

"Maybe he loves her."

Sad at the thought of what it must be like to love someone who could never love them back, Eleanor bowed her head. "I can't imagine. It's a tragedy."

"It is. What a tangled web. Your mother loved your father, but couldn't accept him for who he was, so she married someone else. Your father loved her, but let her go because he knew she couldn't handle his reality. Your adopted father loved your mother, no matter what your aunt says. He would never have married her otherwise and accepted you as his child. Not only that, he raised you as his own. He must have loved you and your mother very much."

A vision of her adopted father, the man who'd raised her, smiling proudly at her college graduation filled her mind's eye. This man was her father. He had raised her, not always perfectly, but he'd loved her and tried his best. Everything he and her mother had done had been out of love, even if they were misguided.

"Do you still want to go to the cemetery?"

Eleanor nodded. She needed to apologize. Their spirits had passed over, but the urge to visit their graves and honor them drove her to go to the last place she'd seen their earthly bodies.

"Hold my hand."

Angela took her hand, and they stepped onto the wet grass in front of her parents' headstones.

Something skittered along her peripheral vision in the darkness. A feeling of foreboding settled on her like a suffocating cloak.

A sibilant whisper shivered through the air. *Eleanor. Come to us, Eleanor.*

Her heart pounded, and she rubbed her suddenly clammy palms on her pants.

Angela grabbed her arm. "Don't listen to them, Eleanor. They have no power over you."

Angry hissing surrounded them.

"Silence," a woman's voice said. "Bring him where she can see him."

"Esme," Angela whispered.

A large male figure stumbled toward them.

"Give me light."

From somewhere, a light appeared, illuminating the figure wavering in front of them.

Eleanor gasped. A sheriff's uniform hung on the emaciated man. Dark hair jutted out haphazardly from his head. Solid black eyes stared blindly from a gaunt face.

"Rodney?"

He didn't answer. He just swayed from side to side.

"Give me the *fesuhn*, and you can have Rodney," Esme said.

"Don't do it, Eleanor." Angela pulled on her arm.

"What choice do I have?"

"If you give it to her, they will get us."

"But if I don't give it to her, he dies."

Rodney collapsed to his knees. Eleanor stepped forward. Angela restrained her. "No. You can't do this."

Eleanor shook her off and took another step toward Esme who smiled and held out her hand, her black eyes glittering with anticipation.

She reached for the clasp at her neck and removed the pendant.

"Eleanor."

She didn't respond to Angela's frantic voice behind her. Instead, she reached out to place it in Esme's. When the *fesuhn* touched Esme's hand, she said, "I give you this *fesuhn* unwillingly."

A loud crackle split the air. The other woman howled and fell to the ground, writhing. The Gehglers screamed in rage.

Eleanor raced over to Rodney. She turned to look at Angela and yelled, "Come on. Let's go."

The Gehglers emerged from the shadows and galloped toward them. Their fangs glowed green in the dark.

Frozen for a second, Eleanor blinked to break the spell, and, with one hand on Rodney and the other on Angela, she took them to safety.

* * * *

They transported into a large open room with a roaring fire in the stove insert. A chocolate brown couch faced the stove. A sturdy, wooden coffee table sat between the couch and the stove. Two oversized, matching chairs were situated just on the other side of the coffee table.

Eleanor led Rodney over to the couch where he collapsed, eyes closed.

"Eleanor." Michael's voice sounded behind them. "What

are you doing here?"

She spun to face him. "I... I didn't know where else to go."

He motioned to Rodney on the couch. "Who's th— Oh, my God! Rodney?"

"He won't answer you. I couldn't leave him with them. I had to bring him along, but, now, I don't know what to do."

"You can't leave him here. They still have control of him. He'll let them in," Michael said.

"I tried to tell her, Michael, but she wouldn't listen to me." Angela put her hand on Eleanor's arm. "You need to let him go."

"No. There must be something I can do." She stepped away from the other woman and sat next to the slumped over Rodney. Leaning forward, she studied his sleeping face. In less than a week, he'd lost several pounds. His cheeks were sunken in. How could something like this happen so quickly? She leaned closer, wracking her brain for a hint of what to do.

His eyes opened. Completely black, they gleamed with a soulless glint. He grabbed her by the throat and squeezed. "Give me the *feshun*. I must have the *fesuhn*."

A sizzle of power sparked, and he yelped. His eyes closed, and he fell back against the couch once again, lifeless.

Eleanor gulped in a breath of air and rolled away from him. Staring up at the ceiling, she breathed deeply. What was she to do? They controlled him. How did she get him back?

"Are you okay?" Michael asked.

Unable to speak, she nodded. His presence brought comfort. She wanted to lean into him and forget about all of this. Instead, she let him help her up and lead her to one of the chairs away from Rodney's comatose form.

"We need to tie him up. I'll get some rope," Michael said.

"No," Eleanor protested, but it came out weak. She knew he was right. Until she could figure out what to do, or Tomani showed her, he had to be tied up. Judging from his condition, he didn't have long before he wasted away.

Chapter Twenty-Five

A few hours later, Michael had left to check on the cattle, leaving the women alone in the house with Rodney. Michael had tied Rodney's hands together and looped the other end of the rope around the leg of the couch to keep him from going anywhere. Eleanor sat at the dining room table where she could still see Rodney, but far enough away she could easily escape should he wake and get loose. Angela sat across from her.

"There's nothing you can do."

"We've gone over this. I have to try. There must be something. If only I knew what to do. If only I could talk to my Itari father. If only..." She sighed in frustration.

"Sometimes, you just have to let go. You can't save everyone."

"He's not just some random person. He was trying to help. If I'd known him long enough, I might've dated him." Her voice hitched on the last couple words.

Angela cupped Eleanor's hand with hers. "Look, I know this is hard."

"You don't—"

"Yes, I do. You think I haven't experienced this before? This isn't the first time they've done this. I've never seen the victim deteriorate so quickly, though. He doesn't have long."

The door opened. Michael walked in. He hung his coat up in the closet and joined the women at the dining room table.

"The activity has increased out there. It's not going to be safe here for much longer." He glanced at the prone figure on the couch.

"If we leave and take Rodney with us, will you be safe here?"

"There are still a few things I can do, but I don't know. I've never seen it like this."

"What if we combine our abilities?" Eleanor asked.

A look passed between Angela and Michael.

135

"This isn't a fantasy novel or a TV show. It's not like that. Angela could put her own wards out, but they wouldn't strengthen mine," Michael said.

"Eleanor." The sibilant whisper slithered through the room.

Everyone jumped and turned toward Rodney. His eyes were open, and he stared at her from the couch. She shivered under his all black gaze. He struggled against his bonds and rolled off the couch. In inchworm fashion, he wiggled toward them, only stopping because of the cord of rope that tethered him. When he couldn't go any further, he snarled.

"Give me the *fesuhn*, Eleanor."

She stared at him, not sure what to do. Forgiveness still eluded her, and time was running out for him. Without that forgiveness, Tomani wouldn't help her. What would she do if she couldn't save Rodney? He writhed against the ropes on the floor, slavering and snarling at them, his solid black eyes devoid of all humanity. One more thing to forgive herself for...if she could. She sighed and blinked back tears. Tears wouldn't help her now.

"You can't save him."

Michael's voice came to her as if from a distance. The two of them seemed to be getting smaller, like she looked down on them from a high above.

He grabbed her arm. "Are you okay?"

She blinked again and quivered, riding a wave of dizziness.

A cackle echoed through the room. Next to the couch, Rodney swayed, standing, his bonds untied at his feet.

"You think you can escape me so easily, Eleanor? Think again." He staggered toward her with a ghoulish leer. "I'll have that *fesuhn* then eat your flesh."

Her heart pounded a rapid tattoo, and she bolted to her feet. Had she made a mistake?

He closed in on them. Michael jumped between the sheriff and Eleanor. Rodney shoved him aside, and Michael slammed into the floor.

Fear surged through her, paralyzing her for a moment. Rodney reached for her when she broke free of her fear, and anger swelled up, replacing it.

"No," she said and shoved her palms toward Rodney. They connected with his shoulders. A burst of energy pulsed out of her and into him. He jerked, his eyes rolled back in his head, and he collapsed on the floor.

Shaking, she dropped down into the chair. Michael moaned and sat up.

"Where did he—"

"Esme," Angela said, interrupting him. "Now do you believe me, Eleanor? We can't keep him here. You can't save him. Rodney is no longer in control of his body. His soul may not even inhabit it any longer. I don't know how he freed himself, but we won't be safe as long as he's here."

"I—"

"No. It's dangerous, potentially deadly. You saw what he did to Michael."

"But I stopped him," she protested.

"This time. What if you're sleeping and he attacks? What then?"

Eleanor didn't have an answer. All of this was her fault. If only she was normal. If only her father had been human. If only...

"Eleanor."

Michael's voice interrupted her morbid thoughts. She raised her gaze to meet his. He knelt next to Rodney. His expression somber, he shook his head.

"He's..." She couldn't finish the sentence.

He nodded.

She rushed to his side and reached for Rodney. Tears welled. How could she have killed him?

"Eleanor," Angela said, "he was no longer alive. Even if his pulse doesn't have a pulse, that doesn't mean he won't wake and come after you."

Something feral rose in Eleanor. Esme wouldn't have him, not even his body. Memories of her father showing her how to heal wounded animals filled her. Desperate, she placed her hands on Rodney's body and visualized pure energy pouring into him, pushing out any of the darkness she saw within him. As the last of the darkness receded, a scream of rage reverberated in her mind. Rodney's chest rose, and he coughed.

"Rodney?"

He opened his eyes. They were brown with whites again. Joy rushed through her. Esme was gone. She'd done it.

"Eleanor," he rasped. He wheezed and labored to breathe. "Thank you," he whispered and squeezed her hand. His chest hitched and stilled, and he stared into space, unseeing.

Frantic, she placed her head on his chest to listen for his heart. Silence.

"No. No. No. You can't die now. I saved you. You can't die. I won't let you."

Ignoring the tears flowing down her face, she began performing CPR on him. Arms wrapped around her from behind, pulling her back. She struggled against them.

"Let me go," she demanded. "I can still save him."

"Eleanor," Michael's deep voice said against her hair, "he's gone. You *did* save him. He can rest in peace now."

"No." She shook her head. "No. He can't die."

"Sshh... He—"

"No, you don't understand. He was trying to save *me* when this happened. It's my fault—"

"There are some things you can't control, no matter how much you wish you could. He was trying to protect you, yes, but this is not your fault."

"You don't understand." Eleanor closed her eyes and bent her head, tears streaming down her face. "You just don't understand."

"I do, sweetheart. I wish I didn't, but I do."

They sat on the floor. He rocked her in his arms, and she curled into him, sobbing against his chest. She'd failed. She'd failed him and herself...and Tomani. Maybe it would've worked if she'd been able to forgive, but she hadn't. She couldn't. She was flawed. Fatally flawed. Nothing would ever change.

Chapter Twenty-Six

Later that evening, Eleanor sat at Michael's dining room table, staring out the window. Everything had quieted down after Rodney's death, as if the Gehglers and Esme were regrouping. Michael had taken Rodney's body outside to bury him. He, Angela, and his brother Garth insisted she stay inside, although she didn't feel much safer inside than she would have outside. After the burial, Angela took a shower and then went to bed. The past few days had exhausted her mentor. Eleanor had stayed at the dining room table, craving the solitude. They seemed to sense her mood and had left her alone.

The fog shifted and swirled outside under the yard light. Although beautiful, it hid a terrifying secret. Out there, the Gehglers waited for them. They waited for them to let their guard down, to be too exhausted to fight anymore. At that moment, giving up looked inviting, and, if she hadn't seen what possession by those creatures did, she might've considered it.

With a sigh, she turned away from the window, away from the yearning for a time before all of this had happened. More people would die if they didn't stop them. But how did they stop them?

Forgive, Eleanor.

She snorted. Forgive. Hadn't she already established she wasn't capable of forgiveness? The one time she'd thought she'd figured it all out ended in the death of an honorable man. She didn't deserve to be forgiven.

Yet, deep inside of her, forgiveness resonated as the answer. Elusive and difficult, it lay just beyond her grasp. Forgiving her parents seemed easy compared to forgiving herself. They had done everything out of fear. Even her father, the one who had raised her, loved her, cared for her, and lied to her, deserved forgiveness. Even Tomani, who refused to help her unless she forgave everyone, could be forgiven. Even her aunt, despite her cursing her, could be forgiven.

The thought of her aunt reminded her of the scene at the cemetery. How had Esme and the Gehglers known to be there? Was it so obvious that she would go there? Had a Gehgler been watching and summoned Esme? No. They'd been there when they arrived. The only people who knew where they were going were her, Angela, and... She looked up with a gasp. Her aunt and uncle. Would her aunt do that? Her heart sank. After her aunt's virulent rant, the possibility of such a betrayal didn't seem so farfetched. Surely, Aunt Shirley couldn't have known what she was doing. Surely...

Her aunt knew. She could tell herself otherwise, but it would be a lie. The betrayal sucked the breath out of her, and she collapsed onto the table, her head resting on her arms. Between her aunt's betrayal and Rodney's death, a desolate, emotional landscape stretched out before her. Could she forgive her aunt? More importantly, could she forgive herself?

Exhaustion seeped into her bones, and she closed her eyes.

"Eleanor." A gentle shaking accompanied the sound of her name. "Eleanor."

She sat up and yawned, rubbing her eyes. Confused for a moment, she blinked. Michael's face came into focus, and the memories poured in. A sob caught in her throat. Strong arms wrapped around her, and she leaned into his warmth. His lips brushed the top of her head.

"Hey." He tucked his finger under her chin and lifted her face up to his. "It's going to be okay."

His beautiful eyes gazed down at her, and she melted. Wanting to forget for a moment, she reached up and pulled his mouth down to hers. Soft and supple, his lips tasted of heaven. His tongue slipped past her lips and into her mouth. Their tongues touched, withdrawing and surging forward in an erotic dance. She moaned and pressed closer to him.

"Eleanor," he whispered against her lips before trailing kisses down her neck.

She let her head fall back, giving him better access to the sensitive skin of her neck. His breath tickled, and she shivered. A thunderous wave of desire roared through her,

140

overloading her senses. Her knees buckled, and he caught her before she slipped to the floor.

He gasped and pulled back just enough for their gazes to meet. Passion smoldered in his eyes, turning them a deep gold. She gasped and, unable—and unwilling—to stop herself, rubbed her aching nipples against his chest. He groaned. Leaning in again, he nipped at her ear. The gasp of pure pleasure that escaped her seemed to egg him on. He slid his hands down her body to cup her butt and ground his erection against her. Liquid heat converged at the juncture of her thighs, and her pussy throbbed with the need to have him inside of her.

"I want you, Michael. Please."

With another groan, he picked her up and carried her to a bedroom. Laying her on the bed with a gentleness that left her impatient, he followed her down and braced himself above her with his arms. He stared at her, his gaze devouring her.

The hunger in his eyes matched the one raging inside her. Reaching up, she unbuttoned his shirt and paused. Hard muscles lightly covered with brown hair beckoned to be touched. The hair trailed down to a vee over washboard abs, drawing her eye to his erection, which strained against his blue jeans. Powerless to stop herself, she ran her hands down the path her gaze had taken.

His abs twitched and rippled under her fingers, and he gasped, his hips bucking into her fingers when she came in contact with his cock.

"Eleanor."

His raspy tone sent shivers down her spine. For the first time in her life, the power of her femininity thrilled her. There had been a few men in the past, but none of them looked at her with the desire reflected in Michael's face, nor did they evoke an answering passion in her. Only Michael stirred the raging inferno inside of her. If he didn't touch her soon, she would self-combust.

As if he heard her thoughts, he lowered himself until the space between their bodies disappeared. For a brief moment, their breath mingled in an intimate pre-kiss, and then his mouth came down upon hers with controlled savagery. Her legs fell open, and she moaned when he nestled between them. She ground her pelvis against his erection, silently urging him to take her.

With a growl, he sat back on his heels and stripped his shirt off. Soft winter light caressed his muscles, and she caught her breath. He reached for his pants' button, but she stopped him.

"Let me," she said, her voice husky with desire.

He nodded, his hand falling away to give her access.

Sitting up, she pushed him over and couldn't contain the smile that slipped across her face. Smug satisfaction filled her that she had done this to him. The fire that burned bright in his eyes, and flushed his cheeks, was for her. She trailed her fingers down his chest, tormenting him.

"Eleanor."

She glanced up at his face. Need was etched on it in stark relief.

"Please, Eleanor."

His plea sent her over the edge. She popped open the button and unzipped his jeans. They slipped them off together. His underwear quickly followed in the wake of his pants, and she paused to drink in the sight of him. A more beautiful man she'd never seen. With his chiseled chest, his six-pack abs, long, muscular legs, and ruggedly handsome face, he could easily be a movie star. And, of course, his cock. Not too big, not too small, the tip touched the skin just below his belly button. She licked her lips. What would he taste like there?

Before she could find out, he started pulling at her clothes.

"You are overdressed," he said. Hunger sparkled in his eyes.

Heat rushed to her cheeks, and, suddenly, uncertainty swamped her. He was so perfect. She—her body—was...not. When he tugged at the hem of her shirt to lift it over her head, she stopped him. Would he still want her once he saw her?

Unable to look at him, she stared at where their hands met, his so masculine against her smaller, feminine ones.

"Eleanor," he said.

She didn't say anything, frozen.

"Eleanor...honey, look at me."

Slowly, she raised her gaze until it connected with his. Understanding mixed with desire in his eyes, and it was incredibly sexy.

He caressed her cheek, and she leaned into his hand.

"You are beautiful, you know."

She shook her head.

"You are, but we don't have to do anything until you're comfortable and trust me. I'd rather we didn't stop, but we can if that's what you want."

Was it what she wanted? Eleanor thought about it. In any other circumstances, they'd be dating now instead of potentially making love. But the heightened sense of danger and their shared experiences had accelerated her feelings for him quicker than normal. Did she love him? Or was it everything else that made her *think* she loved him? And did she need to love him to have sex? If they didn't survive this, she'd never know what could've been. She wanted to know, needed to know. Everything else could wait.

Abandoning her misgivings, she said, "No, I want this. I don't know what'll happen tomorrow, or even tonight, but none of that matters. Only this moment and you matter."

"Are you sure?" he asked.

Instead of answering, she slipped her shirt over her head. Goose bumps raced along her skin when the chilled air hit her. Her nipples strained against her lace bra. His quick intake of breath told her everything she needed to know, and she smiled.

The fesuhn pulsed between her breasts. She'd forgotten its presence and reached to remove it, but his hand stayed hers.

"It can stay."

"Why? How—"

"Our energies are combining, and it knows I'm not a threat. As long as I don't try to take it from you, I will be fine."

"Oh."

He pushed her flat down on the bed, gently moved her hands away from her bra clasp, and bowed his head to suckle

143

on her breasts through the lace. The sensation reignited the banked desire into a blazing inferno. A moan welled up inside of her, escaping through her parted lips. Her pussy clenched with the need to feel him embedded deep within her. Impatient, she slid out from under him and wiggled out of her pants and underwear. Not giving him a chance to see her imperfections, she yanked him close and pressed her naked body against his. The hair on his chest teased her overly sensitive nipples, and she kissed him as if he were her lifeline to keeping her sanity. At that moment, indeed, he was.

"I need you *now*. Inside of me," she said, panting. She squirmed against him, rubbing her pelvis against his cock and moaning.

He groaned, and, without a word, he leaned across her and reached toward the nightstand. A drawer opened and shut. The crinkle of plastic and the sound of ripping echoed in the room. He pulled away to slide the condom on then positioned himself between her legs. Their gazes met. She met his first thrust, her eyes rolling back inside her head. All thoughts of everything else disappeared, except the incredible sensation of him moving in and out of her.

With each thrust of his hips, the tension built inside of her. Fire raced through her veins and spiraled into a tautly wound coil at the juncture of her legs. The coil wound tighter and tighter until she sobbed with the need for release. Then, like a dam bursting, wave after wave of pleasure rolled over her, and she screamed.

A few seconds later, Michael cried his own release and collapsed on top of her.

She smiled, and her eyes drifted closed as she slipped into slumber.

Chapter Twenty-Seven

The cold morning air stung her cheeks. With each breath, a puff of steam appeared before her. Despite the chill, peace filled her battered heart for the first time since her mother's death. She'd come to tell her parents she'd forgiven them, but, as she sat in the quiet, listening to the world awakening around her, the knowledge that they knew and forgave her and loved her as deeply as she loved them flowed through her. Touching the headstone, she smiled.

"Eleanor."

Tomani's voice startled Eleanor. She looked up from where she knelt in front of her mother and father's grave.

"Tomani? What brings you here?" *The question came out an accusation, although she didn't mean it that way.*

"I loved her, you know." *He squatted down beside her, staring at her mother's grave, his face a mask of longing.*

"I know." *Unbidden anger rose within her. Why hadn't he come the other day when she needed him? Now was too late.* "Rodney's gone."

Her words hung heavy in the air between them. He bowed his head.

"I'm sorry, Eleanor. I was forbidden to come. We are not allowed to interfere—"

She waved her hand, cutting him off. "Yes, I know, and a man died because of it."

"But I was proud of you, Leeli. You saved him without any tutoring."

"I didn't save him. He died. I only did what you taught me to do when I was a child with injured animals, but he still died."

Each word came out like a dagger, and he flinched.

"I wouldn't've been able to save him. His body was too ravaged. They'd had him too long. Not even our most practiced healers could've."

"So, you never answered my question. Why are you here?"

145

His shoulders drooped, and Eleanor regretted her harsh words. Rodney's death wasn't his fault. He'd died because of her, not Tomani. All of the anger rushed out of her, leaving her deflated. She touched his shoulder.

"I'm sorry. None of this is your fault."

"It's no one's fault, Leeli. It just is. Sometimes, it just is." He ran his fingers through his hair, frustration evident in every movement. "Look, I didn't come to upset you. I came to tell you that I won't be seeing you again until after everything has been settled with the Gehglers and Esme. The elders fear that I'll interfere if you're in danger, as I have done in the past, so they've forbidden me travel to your universe. They graciously allowed me to come to you this last time now that you know about me." He brushed a strand of hair off of her cheek, tucking it behind an ear, and kissed her forehead.

The sadness in his eyes pierced her soul, and she gasped at the pain she saw in them.

"The key to defeating the Gehglers is forgiveness. You have forgiven your parents and me, even your aunt who betrayed you. Now you must forgive yourself," he said.

He looked over his shoulder. Two beautiful beings stood a few feet behind him.

With a sigh, he rose and helped her up. "Michael is a good man. Trust him. He loves you." He glanced over his shoulder. "Now, I must go. Know I love you and will always love you. Wear your pendant. It will keep you safe."

Before he could turn to go, she threw her arms around him and buried her face in his chest. "I love you, Papa."

His arms wrapped around her, clasping her to him.

"Tomani," one of the beings called.

He brushed a feather light kiss on the top of her head and stepped back. Tears obscured her vision as he turned and joined the others. Their gazes met one more time, and then the Itari disappeared.

Eleanor dropped to her knees and cried.

* * * *

"Eleanor...wake up."

Someone shook her shoulder. Exhausted, Eleanor cracked open grit-filled eyes. Michael leaned over her, a concerned expression on his face.

"Are you okay?"

Unable to speak, she nodded. The dream lingered, a pall weighing her down.

"Do you want to talk about it?" he asked.

She shook her head.

"Okay... May I hold you?"

Without a word, she snuggled into his arms, burying her head against his bare chest. His heart beat a steady, soothing rhythm. In a few minutes, her eyes closed, her breathing slowed, and she drifted off into a restful, dreamless sleep.

Chapter Twenty-Eight

A week passed without any incidents. Eleanor stayed at Michael's. Lily came by to visit, and they retrieved Eleanor's car and the boxes of family pictures from her house. Everything had been torn apart inside the house, although, oddly, they'd left everything in the garage intact. Angela returned to her house when nothing else happened. It appeared that the Gehglers and Esme had given up.

They fell into a routine. Eleanor saw Michael's brother, Garth, at dinner. Preoccupied with school, he chatted briefly each night with them and didn't seem surprised with her being there. While comfortable and easy, the cohabitating with no commitment ate at her. Eleanor had never done this before, and she felt like a guest. She didn't like it at all. She'd had to replace all of her clothes, which now occupied part of Michael's dresser. He didn't seem to mind, but she did. She wanted her own place. While the sex singed her eyebrows, the sense of not knowing what the next day would bring wore on her.

Every night after dinner, and after Garth retreated to his room to study, Eleanor and Michael cuddled on the couch watching the flames dance in the fireplace, her head on his shoulder and his arm around her, and talked. For the first few nights, contentment filled her, but that contentment quickly turned to restlessness. By the seventh day, she couldn't stand it anymore. That night when they sat on the couch, she scooted away and pulled her knees up in front of her, facing him.

"What's wrong?" he asked.

She regarded him in silence. How did she explain the thoughts that swirled in her head?

"I..." She bit her lip and rested her head on her knees. "I don't really know." It wasn't the truth. Well, it was partly true. Returning to her house wasn't a possibility in its current state. Staying here as a guest could only go on for so long. Even if she spent a few nights at Lily's, she'd still be homeless. Her life had spun out of control, and it didn't seem like it was going to change any time soon.

He continued to regard her quietly. His ability to sit and listen without saying anything usually gave her room to collect her thoughts and tell him more, but, tonight, she wanted him to talk. That way, she wouldn't have to. Her feelings could simmer for a bit longer before something had to be done.

He reached out and took her hand. "Whatever you have to say, it's okay. I can't promise to like it, though." He grinned.

She chuckled. "Well, I can't promise you'll like it either. I don't know if *I* like it, but I'm feeling uprooted and helpless. I like that even less."

His smile faded at her words. Understanding dawned in his eyes. "You know you're welcome to stay here for as long as you like, for the rest of your life, if you're so inclined."

Panic rose within her. Her heartbeat pounded loudly in her ears, drowning out her thoughts. Taking a deep breath, she swallowed and attempted to stem the tide that rose up inside of her. She wasn't ready for this. As much as she cared for him and enjoyed being with him, she wanted it on her terms, not because she didn't have a choice. And, at the moment, her choices were limited.

"I... Look..."

"It's not you, it's me, right?" A rueful smile slipped across his rugged features, but it didn't hide the pain that lurked in his eyes.

She frowned, annoyed. "Actually, no. It's this situation. My choices, to some degree, have been taken from me. My house is unlivable, so I'm homeless for the time being." She held her hand up when he looked as if he was going to interrupt her. "Yes, I can stay here with you, but this isn't my home. It's *your* home."

"But—"

The sound of shattering glass interrupted him and brought both of them to their feet.

"Stay here." He strode off toward the kitchen in the direction of the sound.

"Not on your life," she muttered and followed him.

He stopped so abruptly that she ran into his back.

Standing on tiptoe, she looked over his shoulder to see why he'd come to a halt. Lying on the floor in the middle of the kitchen was an odd looking object. It shimmered and sparkled on the oatmeal-colored tile. A humming filled her ears, drowning out everything else, and, in a trance, she pushed Michael out of her way and walked toward the object. When she bent to pick it up, he grabbed her by the arm and pulled her back.

"No, Eleanor," he yelled.

She shook her head and turned to look at him blankly. "Did you say something?"

"Look at me."

"What?" She shook her head again. For some reason, she couldn't think clearly. The most beautiful voice she'd ever heard spun spellbinding melodies inside her head. She wanted to pick up the object, but she couldn't reach it. Something gripped her arm. A part of her mind registered that Michael restrained her. "Let me go," she said, struggling against his hold.

Two strong arms wrapped around her. The voice still sang in her head, calling to her. With the tip of her shoe, she tapped the object. A loud boom ripped through the air, and they flew backward. They connected with something solid, and all of the air rushed out of her. Her lungs burned as she gasped for air.

Winded, she lay without moving on top of Michael, staring at the ceiling. A ringing in her ears replaced the haunting song.

A few minutes later, Michael's voice rasped in her ear. "Eleanor, are you okay?"

Unable to speak, she nodded. She rolled off of him onto the floor, its chill soaking through her clothes. He pulled her close.

They lay on the floor in that position for several minutes, quiescent.

Finally, she sat up and slowly stood. Her body ached all over. "What happened?"

"I don't know. I'm not sure."

She looked at the thing on the floor. Dark and silent, the oval object resembled a piece of unpolished obsidian.

"What is that?" she asked.

"That is a *zirgot*. It's a very powerful, Itari charm. The Itari outlawed them centuries ago. Much like a voodoo doll, it is calibrated to a specific person. As you may have guessed, they're used to control others. Not many Itari know how to make one of these...and for good reason." Worry warred with anger in his eyes. "Esme has help. She isn't powerful enough, old enough, nor knowledgeable enough to create one of these. I'll have to dispose of it and let not only the keepers know, but the Itari."

"I heard it singing the most beautiful song. All I wanted to do was listen to that music forever."

"That's how it gets you. Had you touched it, they would've had you. You would've become like Rodney."

She felt the blood drain from her face, and she swayed. The image of Rodney's gaunt face and black eyes and her inability to help him tormented her still. "But I did touch it."

"You did?"

"Yes, with my toe."

"Why didn't it work?"

Without thinking, she reached up and touched the *fesuhn*. It pulsed against her hand.

Comprehension lit his face followed quickly by a thoughtful look. "They know you have the *fesuhn*. It protects against all and any attacks. Why would they bother with something like this unless..." His voice trailed off, and he snatched up the lifeless *zirgot*. "We need to turn this over to the Itari now."

"How?" How did one travel to parallel universes?

He grabbed her hand and pulled her through the house. At the end of the hallway, he stopped and moved the area rug aside to reveal the hardwood floor. With the touch of his hand, the floor slid to one side. It was a hidden door. A packed dirt staircase led down into the darkness.

"Garth," he called.

His brother stuck his head out of his room. "What's going on?"

"A *zirgot*."

Garth's eyes widened. Without a word, he came out of his room, textbook in hand, and ran down the stairs, lights flickering to life under his feet.

"Come on," Michael said to Eleanor and rapidly descended the steps.

Eleanor hesitated. Considering everything that had happened the past few weeks, a hidden staircase was minor. But to descend into the earth, into the unknown, evoked some primal fear.

He paused to look over his shoulder at her. "We don't have much time."

His words snapped her out of her momentary paralysis, and she hurried down after him. Part way down, the door slid closed behind her. Startled, she spun. The stairs above her were dark. Eyes wide, she turned and raced after Michael and Garth. His brother had already disappeared. Several feet away now, Michael trotted down the stairs. They curved to the left, and he disappeared around the bend. With a burst of speed, she rounded the corner and stumbled when the steps came to an end in a large, bright room.

No sooner did she clear the stairs than a whoosh sounded behind her. She jumped and glanced over her shoulder. A solid rock wall greeted her. All trace of the staircase had disappeared. She turned back to the room.

In the far corner, a door led off to somewhere. Garth sat in one of the two recliners that faced a large couch in the same brown leather, separated by a glass coffee table. Michael was striding across the room to a large island. Beyond the island were a fridge, a stove, some cabinets, and a sink.

"Why did we come down here? Where are we?"

"This is a safe room, protected by wards, protected from Gehglers, and impenetrable by other powers as well," he said. "We haven't had a reason to use it, but we do now. Esme, and whomever she is dealing with, know about your *fesuhn*. The *zirgot* drained a lot of the pendant's power when it protected you. It'll take some time for it to regenerate, making you vulnerable to an attack. This is why I brought you here. You'll be safe down here for the time being. I must get this to the Itari."

"Wait! You're leaving me here? Alone?"

"You won't be alone. Garth'll be here."

Panic skittered through her. "How long will you be?"

"Overnight."

"Overnight?" Her heart pounded, and she rubbed her suddenly sweaty palms on her jeans. "Why so long? What if I have to leave? What if I can't stay down here?" The walls started closing in again. The blood drained from her head, and the room spun.

He closed the distance between them and gently gathered her in his arms. With a kiss on the top of her head, he said, "Hey, you'll be fine. I won't be gone long, and Garth is here." He stepped away. "The fridge is stocked, there are dishes in the cabinets, and there's running water. Through that door," he pointed to a door she hadn't seen when she'd first walked in, "is a bathroom." He motioned to the door she'd seen. "That door leads to the bedrooms."

Chapter Twenty-Nine

I won't be gone long. The phrase repeated in her head like a mantra. As comfortable as they'd made this underground living space, it still didn't have any windows, nor could she leave. If she thought about it too much, the walls closed in on her.

She sat on the couch and stared at the coffee table. For the first time, she noticed the magazines and a large photographic book of big cats. She picked it up and started thumbing through it. Some of the photos took her breath away. Their eyes pierced through her. They were such beautiful, deadly animals.

There was only so long she could study the photos, though. Soon, she returned the book to the coffee table and picked up another one. An hour or so later, she'd exhausted her reading options and found herself faced with nothing to do but think. Think about where she was, what she faced, and what she'd been charged to do. Her father's words ran through her head. *The key to defeating the Gehglers is forgiving yourself.*

She laughed. He said it as if it were easy. All of those self-help books adjured one to look inside. Years of looking inside had revealed nothing. Forgiveness still eluded her.

But what do you have to forgive, Eleanor? Her father's voice whispered in her mind. *What is the great sin you've committed that you can't forgive yourself for? Other than Rodney, which you had no control over, what have you done that deserves your wrath?*

The questions made her pause. What did she have to forgive herself for? There were so many times she wished she could change her reaction or her words. Or, better yet, she'd love to erase an entire event because her actions embarrassed her. And, besides Rodney, her biggest transgression was her anger at her mother for leaving her alone, for dying of cancer. It had been different with her father. For some reason, she hadn't felt abandoned by him. He had to go. But with her mother... Even though she knew her mother couldn't change what was happening, and she knew her anger wasn't logical, she couldn't resolve her feelings of being abandoned. She'd forgiven her mother, but how did she forgive herself for being angry at something her mother couldn't control and herself for not being able to control her anger? Her mother had needed her daughter's support, love, and understanding, not her anger.

"How? How do I forgive myself for *that*?" she whispered.

Her mother's death loomed in front of her, and the pain of loss stabbed at her again. A sob wracked her body. Too tired to fight them, she allowed the tears to run their course until the last sniffle faded.

How long she sat hunched over staring blindly at the dirt wall on the other side of the room she didn't know, but when she moved to stand, her muscles protested. Mother Nature called and then bed. Perhaps a good night's sleep would help her find the answers.

* * * *

"Eleanor?"

The fog of sleep slowly lifted, and she opened her eyes. Michael's tired face came into focus. She smiled and reached up to caress his cheek.

"You're back."

His answering smile warmed his eyes. "I am. Do you have room for me?"

With a nod, she scooted over. He stripped and slid into bed beside her. He slipped his arms around her, and she snuggled into his embrace. A contented sigh escaped her lips as she drifted back to sleep.

* * * *

Tingles shivered down her spine, goose bumps popping up in their wake. A soft moan whooshed out of her, and she squirmed under the teasing onslaught. Hands encircled her breasts, squeezing her nipples. She thrust her hips back against the hard male body behind her.

"Open for me."

His breath tickled her ears, sending a new set of shivers coursing down her spine. Eyes closed, she obeyed his command and gasped when his hard, covered length slid into her. She vaguely wondered when he'd put a condom on, but such thoughts disappeared as desire shot through her veins. His lips on her neck, one hand toying with a nipple, the other working her clitoris, and his cock stroking in and out of her from behind sent her over the edge. An orgasm crashed over her, and she cried out his name. A few more thrusts, and he groaned his release against her neck. He pulsed inside of her and then stilled.

Serenity swirled around her, and Morpheus's realm claimed her.

* * * *

Mist swirled around her feet. In the distance, a coyote yipped, followed by a chorus of its pack mates. Eleanor shivered and rubbed her chilled arms. What was she doing out here? Michael had told her never to come here alone.

Something rustled in the brush behind her, and she spun. Solid black eyes stared at her out of an emaciated child's face. Lank, black hair hung in matted strands on either side of its face. A long, snake-like tongue flicked out and licked its lips.

"Eleanor," it whispered, "come to me."

With a shake of her head, she stepped back. "No."

It hissed. "Give it to me, Eleanor," it demanded.

She retreated another step. "No."

"Give it to me," it screamed and launched itself at her.

With a jolt, Eleanor awoke. Her heart pounding, she stared at the ceiling. Next to her, Michael slept, his steady breathing spoke of a deep, dreamless sleep. In the dark, windowless room, day and night meant nothing.

Part of her wanted to wake him and bury her head in his chest, but she wouldn't. Instead, she stared wide-eyed into the darkness, telling herself it was just a dream, waiting for the fear to abate, and hoping she'd fall back into a dreamless sleep.

But sleep didn't come. Her mind churned with images of the Gehgler, its open mouth full of fangs and dagger-like claws reaching for her. The pendant glowed against her chest, a faint light in the pitch-black room.

Michael stirred beside her. Covering the *fesuhn*, she forced herself to focus on something, anything, else. It pulsed in her hand, and light spilled out from between her fingers in beams until the entire room was lit in stark relief. In that light, two women and one man appeared at the foot of the bed in soft, gray cloaks. The hoods of their cloaks rested on their shoulders, revealing faces of unearthly beauty—high cheekbones, broad brows, full lips, and almond-shaped eyes. A pale blue glow emanated from them. The woman in the center motioned to the others, who raised their hoods. Her silver eyes bespoke of wisdom and otherworldly knowledge.

Michael sat up, the blanket pooling about his waist. "Sharhon, what brings the three of you here?"

Sharhon's eyes narrowed, the corners of her mouth turning down. "The elders are concerned and have changed their minds. She's causing too much trouble here. If it's not resolved soon, we'll have to interfere."

Michael tensed. Eleanor moved to sit, but remembered she was nude. Holding the covers to her chest, she stared at the intruders.

"What do you mean 'interfere'?" she asked.

Sharhon's gaze pierced her. "We will have to do something we haven't done in centuries. All because of *you*."

She turned to Michael. "What does she mean?"

"Your presence and your *fesuhn* have incited the Gehglers. They are popping up all over the world, creating havoc."

"It can't continue without disrupting the evolution of your mother's species," Sharhon said to Eleanor. "That you exist is forbidden—and you can see why interbreeding between our species is not allowed—but you *do* exist. Now we must deal with the consequences."

"O...kay..." She glanced at Michael and then back at the three beings. "I—"

"You have seven days to fix this. If you don't, we will."

Sharhon flipped her hood over her head, and they disappeared.

Eleanor turned to Michael filled with foreboding. "What did she mean? How will they fix this?"

"You'll be taken to Itar and put on trial, along with your father," he said.

Trial? For being born? "And if we're found guilty?"

"You'll die."

Michael's words hit her with the force of a blow, and the air rushed out of her. Eyes wide, she regarded him in shock. Death. If the Gehglers didn't get her, the Itari would...unless she solved the problem. Which meant forgiving herself—in one week—and somehow banishing them.

Hysterical laughter bubbled up and spilled out of her. The laughter dissolved into tears and finally hiccups.

Raising a tear-streaked face to Michael, she asked, "What am I to do?"

"What did your father tell you to do?"

Surprise flitted through her. "You know?"

"I knew the moment I saw you."

"How?"

"Because I am Itari. My entire family is. Don't you remember? We talked about this."

Eleanor nodded. Their conversation from the day she'd fled San Antonio came flooding back to her. How had she forgotten? So much had been going on, and she'd buried it, not wanting to acknowledge what she'd known all along—he wasn't of this world and was beyond her reach.

"Why don't you look like them? And why are you here?"

"My family monitors this plane for the Itari. We have been here for the past three generations. My family was chosen for our resemblance to humans."

"You've broken the rules."

"Yes."

"Why?"

"Because I couldn't *not* break them." He reached up and cupped her cheek. "I would die for you, Eleanor. I love you." He leaned in and kissed her.

She fell into his embrace, her defenses crumbling as she admitted, if only to herself, that she loved him, too.

Chapter Thirty

That first day they spent underground, it had taken several hours to bring the temperature up to what Eleanor deemed livable. She had spent most of that day huddled by the fireplace, hands outstretched, or snuggled under a down blanket. Michael had gone out and checked on the cattle and the outlying buildings. One or two cows were missing, but whether that was from the Gehglers or wild animals, he wasn't sure. All things considered, they'd escaped fairly unscathed.

After the first day, he led her up into the house. Other than open doors, nothing was out of place. According to Michael, the Gehglers couldn't stand the type of energy within the house. But, just in case of an emergency, and if no one else was home, he showed her how to access the bunker. He also gave her a lesson in resisting *zirgots* should they try such a tactic again. So far, they hadn't.

To keep from having too much time to think, Eleanor helped Michael with his chores, cleaned house, and prepared meals—something she'd never liked. Jennifer would laugh if she saw her. Eleanor, the domestic diva. She snorted. She still didn't care for cleaning or cooking, but she would go stir crazy with worry.

Despite the passage of time and the busy work, Eleanor found herself no closer to forgiving herself. The clock was ticking. She either discovered the magic secret, or all of them died.

During a break from chores that afternoon, she sat in the living room. A cheery fire danced in the fireplace, in direct contrast with her mood. If it matched her mood, black flames would flicker and consume the wood in seconds. She ran her hand through her hair and leaned her head back against the couch. Four more days before the Itari returned. Four days to get her act together.

Frustration built, forcing her to stand. Sitting around thinking about not being able to solve the problem wouldn't change anything. It was time to do something different. She headed toward the kitchen where she'd plugged in her phone.

Michael came in from outside. "Who're you calling?"

She smiled. "Lily. I could use some advice."

He raised an eyebrow. "I'm here if you want to talk."

"I... I just want to talk to another woman." And it was true. As much as she loved him, she needed another woman's perspective.

"Why don't you invite her over for tea?"

She eyed him. Tea meant all of them sitting around together. He would put in his two cents. She opened her mouth, but he stopped her.

"I have chores to do around the ranch anyway. You two can have the house to yourselves and talk about," he waved his hand, "whatever women talk about." His eyes twinkled.

With a laugh, she said, "Oh, all right. Tea here."

A quick call, and Lily was driving over. A few minutes later, the doorbell rang.

Eleanor answered the door with a grin.

Lily's cheerful face greeted her. "Well, it's been a while. Finally coming up for air, huh?"

Heat rushed to her cheeks. "Why don't you come in," she said, ignoring Lily's comment.

"That's the way of it, I see."

Too embarrassed to say anything, she led Lily into the kitchen where the teapot warmed on the stovetop. Teacups waited in saucers on the counter. "What type of tea do you want? He has Earl Grey, organic Chai, peppermint, and orange twist."

"Peppermint, please." She leaned against the counter and studied Eleanor, all humor and teasing disappeared. "So, why did you call?"

Eleanor put the teabag in the cup and poured boiling water over it. "Sugar? Honey?"

Lily shook her head. "No, thanks."

Handing the cup and saucer to Lily, she repeated the process for herself before answering her friend's question, "I need your advice." Cup in hand, she walked back to the living room, set her cup and saucer on the coffee table, and sat on the couch.

Lily followed her and sat down on the other end of the couch. Taking a sip, she looked at Eleanor over the rim of her cup. She set the saucer on the coffee table and wrapped her hands around the cup. Settling into the couch, she kicked off her shoes, tucked her feet under her, and asked, "What kind of advice?"

"How do you forgive yourself?" Eleanor blurted out.

Her normally bubbly friend frowned. "For what?"

"For everything."

"Honey, you can't forgive yourself for everything. You aren't responsible for everything, only yourself."

Eleanor hung her head and closed her eyes. "I know." Looking up, she met Lily's troubled gaze. "But how do you forgive yourself when someone dies because of you? For being angry at a loved one as they are dying? For being stupid?"

Lily placed the cup in the saucer and leaned forward to grab Eleanor's hand. "First, if you are talking about Rodney, his death isn't your fault." Eleanor opened her mouth to protest, but Lily held up her hand and stopped her, a distant expression in her eyes. "Many years ago, when I was in college, I was supposed to go with some friends to a party. We were meeting at Gemma's place at exactly 7 p.m. I was supposed to be the designated driver. But on the way there, my car broke down, and they left without me. Gemma was driving when a car careened through a stop sign and T-boned them. All of them died." She paused, her voice catching on the last few words.

"After the crash, I blamed myself. My best friends were dead, and it was my fault. If only I'd been driving... If only I'd been with them..." She sighed and smiled sadly. "My mother took me aside one day and asked me if anything would've changed if I'd been there? For me, the change would've been my death and my parents would've been mourning me, too. At that moment, I realized I couldn't have saved them. And my friends wouldn't want me to blame myself." She squeezed Eleanor's hand. "Could you have stopped what happened to Rodney?"

"I—" Could she have? At that moment in time? No. The Gehglers would've gotten her, too. Yes, he was there because

161

of her, but her being there wouldn't have altered what happened to him. Something clicked with that realization. A sigh slipped through her lips, and all of the guilt and anger she'd harbored about his death evaporated. "Thank you."

"As for your mother's death—"

"How did you know it was my mother?"

"You told me about it. Anger is part of the grieving process. It's a human response. And you had started grieving even as she was dying. You knew she was dying, didn't you?"

Although it wasn't a question, Eleanor answered with a nod. She had known. As soon as her mother told her the diagnosis, she'd known it was a death sentence. For the next year, she'd watched her mother slowly deteriorate until she was nothing but a shell of the woman who'd raised her. And she'd been angry at her mother, angry at the disease, angry at the doctors for not being able to do more, and angry at the world. The anger had left, but the grief and guilt remained.

"Even if you're half Itari, you're still half human. Your anger was a natural response. Would your mother want you to be angry at yourself for being human?"

No, but her mother would've instructed her to ask God for forgiveness. But whether God forgave her or not wouldn't affect whether she forgave herself.

"Only you can decide to forgive yourself. Because you're human and not perfect, you're bound to make mistakes. All of us do. Not forgiving yourself prevents you from growing and learning. It's also an excuse. If you're constantly wallowing in self-pity or anger at yourself, nothing changes." Lily took a sip of her tea before asking, "What do you gain from not forgiving yourself?"

Anger welled up inside of her, and derision laced her voice when she said, "Gain?" She snorted. "I gain nothing."

"Oh, no, you gain something from it. Or you did. Maybe you don't anymore, but you still aren't willing to let it go, which means you're holding onto something, or you'd just do it."

"So, you're saying that all I have to do is *decide* to forgive myself. Boy, I wish I'd known *that* all along."

"You asked me. That's what I've found to be true for me. But, you know, if you don't want to forgive yourself, life will continue as is."

A pit opened in Eleanor's stomach, and all of the anger dissolved. "Actually, no, it won't."

"Oh, yes, it will," Lily said.

"No, it won't. I have to defeat the Gehglers in four days or the Itari will come do it. If they have to interfere, my father and I, and possibly Michael, will have to face the consequences."

Lily paled. "Eleanor...no... I..."

Eleanor closed her eyes. Defeat tasted bitter. Unlike Lily, she couldn't just "decide" to forgive herself. It didn't work that way. Did it? But what if Lily was right about this? What did she gain from the guilt and pain and anger? According to her father, she'd never master her full powers if she held onto it. Only mastery, or at least access, to her full powers would make it possible to defeat the Gehglers. How was not having full control of her powers a gain? And why did her full powers rest on forgiveness?

Her head ached with all of the unanswered questions. Rubbing her temples, she concentrated on her breathing. It was all too much. Why couldn't her father just have told her what to do?

Chapter Thirty-One

After Lily left, Eleanor cleaned the shower for the sixth time in three days. The oatmeal-colored tile gleamed, not a speck of mold or dirt in the grout remained, and the glass door was so clear Michael had already walked into it once. She leaned back on her haunches in a crouch and swiped the back of her hand across her forehead, pushing her bangs out of her eyes. Even she had to admit her efforts were wasted on the shower. She regarded the floor. Spotless. A bit frantic, she looked around the rest of the bathroom for something to clean. Anything to keep her occupied.

"Did you clean like this at your house?"

She jumped at the sound of Michael's voice. Turning to face him, she said, "No."

He held his hand out to her. "Come here."

She took it and let him help her up. Prickles invaded her calves and feet as blood rushed back into them. "Ouch."

"So, what's up?"

Frowning, she shrugged. The questions her conversation with Lily had raised swirled in her head and muddied her thoughts. "I don't know."

He raised an eyebrow at her, wry humor twinkled in his eyes. "Really?"

She averted her gaze to stare at the scrub brush in her hands. "I... I'm not ready to talk about it."

"All right."

He lifted the scrub brush out of her hands and set it on the counter then took her glasses off and set them next to the scrub brush. Encircling her with his arms, he asked, "You want to take a shower with me?"

His husky voice sent shivers down her spine, and she melted into his embrace. Liquid heat pooled at the juncture of her thighs, and she nodded, lifting her face to meet his seeking lips. He slid his hands down to her butt and squeezed, pulling her against him. His erection pressed against her stomach as their tongues clashed in a passionate duel.

He pulled back with a groan. "You turn the shower on. I'll get the condom," he rasped.

The rampant desire in his eyes electrified the storm raging inside of her. Unable to speak, she nodded. With shaking hands, she turned to the shower and twisted the knob on. She pulled her shirt over her head and set it on the counter. Unclasping her bra, she let it drop on top of her shirt. She was reaching for her pants when Michael's hands encircled her breasts. He pinched her nipples, and her knees wobbled.

"I love how your breasts fill my hands," he said.

Teeth nipped at the tender skin of her neck. Liquid fire raced through her blood. She relaxed, her head falling back onto his naked chest, and moaned. Anxious to get him inside of her, she tugged at her pants. He grabbed her hands and spun her to face him. Quickly unzipping her pants, he slipped them down her legs. He knelt at her feet and looked up at her, his eyes half-closed and a seductive smile lifted the corner of his mouth.

She licked her lips at the sight of his engorged cock, already covered with a condom, jutting out from his body. With a groan, he hooked his fingers around her lace underwear and yanked them down. They gathered at her feet, trapped by her pants and shoes. He nudged her back, and the backs of her knees connected with the toilet, upsetting her balance. She sat with a plop on the toilet lid.

Her eyes widened when he spread her legs, edged her butt forward, and ducked his head to claim her with his mouth. His tongue flicked her clitoris, and an avalanche of sensations cascaded over her. One finger slid into her, followed quickly by another, while he worked her clitoris with his tongue. Trapped and bombarded by an ever-increasing build up of desire, she shattered into a million pieces.

He lapped at her juices and then, suddenly pulling her shoes, pants, and socks off in one move, he picked her up and stepped into the shower with her.

She didn't think she could come again after such a strong climax. "Michael, I—"

He covered her mouth with his, silencing her, and pressed her back against the cold shower tile as he slid into her. She entwined her legs with his and rode him. With each thrust, her back pressed against the cool wall and he slammed into her, filling her to the hilt and teasing her clit.

The scent of their desire swirled around them in the steamy air. It was earthy, intoxicating, and awakened a primal need to come. A ball of energy spiraled down her into her pussy. Her core tightened, her nipples peaked, and she screamed when her climax crashed over her. Another pump, and he pulsed inside of her.

His forehead rested against hers, his breathing ragged, he chuckled. "So much for the shower."

She let her legs slide down his until her feet touched the floor. "Now, we can clean up leisurely."

"Mmm..." He kissed her gently on the lips. "That would be nice."

He slipped out of her and reached for the soap. Lathering up his hands, he gave her the bar and proceeded to wash her, starting at her shoulders. He lingered on her breasts and skimmed her belly. Slipping one hand between her legs, he gently cleansed her sensitive pussy. He pushed her under the spray and rinsed her off, tweaking her nipples.

She moaned and pushed him back. "None of that, or you'll be in trouble."

Desire sparked in his eyes. "I'm okay with that."

She looked down at his dick. It was rising again. "Yes, I see that you are, but we'd need another condom."

He pulled off the used one and tied off the top. He set it in a corner before turning back to her. Raising his arms out to the side, he said, "I'm all yours. But be warned, this could get you just what you are looking for."

Mischief bubbling up, she said with a grin, "A nice cuddle and massage?"

He tilted his head back and laughed.

His laughter turned into a gasp when her soapy hands wrapped around his cock. She caressed him as she washed off the evidence of their union. Her ministrations bore fruit, and he grew until he was completely erect.

He groaned. "Eleanor..."

Water sluiced down him, rinsing the suds away. She licked her lips, and, before he could stop her, she took him

166

into her mouth. He tasted of soap with a hint of musk and Michael. Her pussy clenched with the need to feel him inside of her again, but she wanted him to come in her mouth this time. She'd never wanted to taste a man's cum, but she did his. Sitting on her heels, she sucked his erection and rubbed her clit on the back of her foot at the same time. His cock stiffened further under the vibrations of her moans.

"Oh, my God, Eleanor," he gasped, grabbing her head and pushing himself deeper into her mouth, "what are you doing?"

Without replying, she continued to suck while she pumped his dick and bounced ever so slightly on her heel. Her breath quickened, and desire coiled within her, winding tighter and tighter until it sprung loose. As her orgasm exploded over her, she reflexively sucked harder.

He groaned and spurted into her mouth. She swallowed and discovered she loved it. Creamy and smooth, it was a mixture of sweet and salty. Not at all like she'd imagined. Perhaps Itari cum tasted different from humans'. After he finished, she licked her lips.

If they survived, she'd be doing this again.

Chapter Thirty-Two

The sexual encounter in the shower renewed Eleanor's desire to live. She wanted a future with Michael. To do that, she had to tackle forgiveness. Avoiding it wasn't going to make it happen, nor was there going to be an epiphany while scrubbing the tiles. Well, maybe scrubbing the tiles if Michael joined her. She chuckled, and happiness bubbled up inside of her.

Yes, this was what she wanted for her life—these moments of happiness.

A walk outside would help, but not here. And the use of energy to jump ley lines from the house might draw more Gehglers. They might not be able to follow her, but the presence of an army of them outside would create more problems. The bunker. The bunker would hide her from them. She could leave from there.

Walking down the hall, she activated the switch and waited for the door to slide open. With quick steps, she descended the stairs. The door clicked shut behind her, and, she continued down around the bend to the main room. Once in there, she looked around. It was empty. Michael had come down here some time ago. Was he in one of the bedrooms?

"Michael?" she called.

No one answered.

She frowned and crossed to the door leading to the bedrooms and entered the hall. The lights flickered on, revealing the five doors, two on either side and one at the end. The last time she'd been there, she'd been so exhausted she hadn't explored, only gone into the first room on the right and climbed into bed. She opened the first door on the left—the one she and Michael had stayed in those first few days. The room was identical to the one on the right with its king-sized bed, two nightstands, recessed lighting, taupe walls, and a few framed landscapes to give the illusion of windows. A connecting door led to an en suite bathroom. She checked the next room on the left and then the other on the right. The

168

rooms were pretty much the same. Each was empty. That left the last door at the end of the hallway.

Uncertainty welled up inside of her. The last door most likely was another bedroom, but suddenly it loomed in front of her, an unknown entity growing more ominous with each passing second. As her hand touched the knob, energy zipped through her, and she paused. With a deep breath, she opened the door.

Warm air wafted past her. A whisper of power skittered down her spine, raising goose bumps all over her body. She rubbed her arms and shut the door behind her before turning back to the room, curious.

Hidden lights illuminated a large cavern. In one corner, a waterfall spilled over some rocks down into a small pool. The water flowed off into a wall, disappearing with a burble. A large flower carved out of an opalescent stone emitted a pale blue glow from the far side of the room.

Drawn to the sculpture, she crossed the room to it. With each step, the intensity of the energy increased until her entire body tingled. Upon reaching it, she placed her right hand on the flower. A low, ethereal humming filled her head, and a jolt shot through the center of her palm, up her arm to spread through her body. The *fesuhn* pulsed where it rested against her chest.

She pulled her hand back, and the humming ceased. Puzzled, she stared at her palm. She'd expected a mark, but it looked the same. Opening and closing her fingers, she studied her hand. It seemed the same, but she felt different. Something had changed.

She frowned and touched the flower again, trying to decipher what had happened. Power rippled over her, caressing her. The humming buzzed on her nerve endings, and words began forming in her mind.

"Eleanor?"

Michael's voice broke the spell, and she snatched her hand back, rubbing it against her pants.

"What are you doing?"

She turned. "I was looking for you."

He walked toward her. "Down here?"

With a shrug, she put some distance between her and

the stone. Tendrils of power swirled around her, beckoning to her. She fisted her right hand.

"You said you were coming down here."

"That was hours ago."

"Yes, well..." She struggled to find the words, the sculpture still drawing her focus.

"Why don't we go back upstairs?" He reached for her arm.

Shaking her head, she pulled away from him. "No. I came down here to tell you I need to go for a walk, to get out, to clear my head."

"You can't go out there."

"I don't mean out *there*." She motioned upward. "Somewhere without the Gehglers. I can't think anymore, and I don't have long to figure this out." Panic rose inside her, curling around her lungs, shortening her breath. She looked at her hands as if seeing them for the first time. They clasped and unclasped of their own accord. With concerted effort, she stilled them and drew in a shaky breath, forcing the panic back down.

"Hey," he said, wrapping his arms around her, "you'll get it done. I have faith in you."

Desperation clawed at her. She shook her head. "You don't understand—"

"I understand you're scared. It will come—"

"I have four—no, almost three—days left. If I don't figure this out—"

"But you will," he assured her.

She pulled back to look on his beloved face. Their gazes met. "What if I don't?" she whispered. "What if I don't and we die?"

Confidence poured out of him and into her. "But you will. You're on the verge, Eleanor. You just push through it. Look within, and you'll find it. Sometimes, it's just a matter of deciding."

She narrowed her eyes at him. "That's what Lily said."

"Well, Lily's a very wise woman." He clasped her elbow and led her toward the door. "Now, why don't we go back upstairs?"

Irritation mounted within her. She wasn't a child and

didn't care to be treated like one. "I don't *want* to go upstairs. I *want* to go for a walk."

"Running away won't bring you any closer to your answers. You can find them anywhere. You have to be open to them."

Tamping down her simmering anger, she tried again. "Look, I'm feeling trapped. I can't think when I feel trapped. I haven't been out of this house for more than three days. Down here, I could use the ley lines and go some place where the Gehglers can't reach me. Even five minutes would help."

He studied her for a moment and then a smile broke across his face. "I know exactly where to go. You will be safe there." He held his hand out to her.

Suspicious, she crossed her arms and stared at him. Where could that possibly be? Itar?

"Come on. You'll enjoy it." When she didn't respond, he raised an eyebrow at her, his eyes twinkling. "Have I ever done anything to make you suspicious of me?"

"No."

"Then take my hand. I promise, you'll enjoy yourself."

With one last glance at the flower, she said, "Oh, all right," and took his hand.

A blink of an eye later, they stood on a wooden pier crowded with people. Families, couples, groups chattered in several different languages. Bundled up in winter clothes, vendors hawked their wares, artists created masterpieces, wowing anyone who stood long enough to watch, and psychics promised to tell their future for a mere five dollars. A Ferris wheel, with its rainbow of lights, spun near the end of the pier. There was even a small rollercoaster.

Cold, moist air stung her cheeks. She shivered and wished for her coat, but being outside exhilarated her. A weight lifted off her chest, and she breathed deeply of the salty sea air. High overhead, stars twinkled in an inky expanse of sky.

"Where are we?" she asked.

"The Santa Monica pier," he said. He grabbed her hand. "Come. Let's go to the end and look out over the ocean."

She shivered. "It's cold."

"Do you want to go back now?"

"Oh, no," she smiled, "I can handle a bit of cold."

He grinned at her. They walked down the pier, surrounded by humanity, and Eleanor couldn't contain the joy that leapt within her. With a bounce in her step, she grinned. Soon, it would end, but, for the moment, she would revel in this small freedom and forget about the future.

At the end of the pier, the ocean stretched out before them. People leaned against the railing, and she joined them, letting the negative ions uplift her already buoyant mood. Love welled up inside of her for this amazing man. Turning to him, she stood on her tiptoes and kissed his cheek.

Michael looked down at her and smiled, his face half in shadow. "What was that for?"

"For bringing me here, for understanding, for... everything," she said.

The lines around his eyes softened, and love shone in them. "You're welcome," he said and pulled her into his embrace.

She caught her breath and encircled his waist with her arms. How could she give this up? And it finally hit her that she couldn't. The time had come. If she wanted this life—him, she had to forgive herself. She returned her gaze to the black water. Waves crashed underneath them, a soothing, rhythmic sound beating a counterpoint to her accelerated pulse.

With Michael's arm wrapped around her, she whispered over and over, "I forgive. I forgive. I forgive."

Chapter Thirty-Three

Free of the burden of guilt and anger, Eleanor felt lighter and defeating the Gehglers didn't seem so impossible anymore. How she would do it, she didn't know, but she could. She shivered and snuggled deeper into Michael's embrace.

He kissed the top of her head and said, "Why don't we go get some dinner? There's a restaurant at the top of the pier that makes a delicious Boston clam chowder."

At the mention of food, her stomach growled. Her eyes widened, and she giggled. "I guess I'm hungry."

Arms around each other, they strolled through the crowds to the restaurant. Over dinner, they shared stories of their lives. He regaled her with ones of Itar, his parents and brothers, and working the ranch. She told him of her childhood, her family, her college days, and her job before her parents' deaths. Someday, she hoped to meet his family. He would never meet hers, but she'd introduce him to her best friend Jennifer. After all of this was done, she'd have to call her.

"Well, I think it's time to return to the ranch," he said.

She sighed and nodded. Reality intruded. "It's been so lovely."

He reached over and caressed her hand, smiling. "We'll have many more nights like this. I promise."

"Don't make promises you can't keep." She smiled sadly.

His expression turned serious. "I don't make promises lightly. We *will* have more evenings. This I vow."

He was promising to interfere, and she couldn't let him do that. The repercussions could be fatal.

"I must do this alone, Michael. The rules say so."

He scowled. "No, you can't. I—"

She touched his arm and stared into his face, beseeching him to do as she asked. "I must when it comes to facing them, but perhaps you can help me in other ways. My knowledge of the Gehglers is limited beyond the few times I've run into them. Then there is Esme. Other than my encounter with her in the graveyard, I know nothing about her. You can share their weaknesses with me and anything else you can think of."

He opened his mouth as if to say something then clamped it shut.

"Promise me," she said.

He turned his face away and looked at the people milling around them.

"Michael," she said and waited for him to return his attention to her, "promise me."

Sadness lurked in his eyes. "I can't."

"Then I'll have to go somewhere else, somewhere you won't know where I am." She touched his cheek and walked away from him.

"Eleanor," he called from behind her.

She didn't turn around, but continued toward a dimly lit area. Fast approaching footsteps sounded behind her. A hand on her shoulder stopped her.

"All right," he said, "I'll do as you ask, but know it's under duress."

Relief spilled through her, and her shoulders slumped. She faced him. Wrapping her arms around his waist and leaning her head on his chest, she breathed in his scent and snuggled closer. "Thank you."

He rested his head on the top of hers. "We're in this together, you know." He stepped back and took her hand. "Now, let's go back. We have a battle to plan."

Battle. She hadn't thought of it as a battle, but it was, except it wasn't two large forces at war. It was her against a legion of Gehglers and God knew what else.

"All right."

The air shimmered in front of them, and they stepped through to the cavern of the bunker. Almost immediately, the stone in the corner hummed, drawing their attention.

She turned toward it and asked, "What is that?"

"It is a *somel*, a power stone. There are a few of these placed throughout this plane. It's a link to Itar, which is why Sharhon was able to come to us, and much more. It's part of the reason the Gehglers don't like the energy in the house, and yet they are drawn to it."

"Can it be drained like the *fesuhn*?"

He shook his head. "No."

"If the Gehglers or Esme got a hold of it, would they be able to use its powers?"

"At one time, Esme could've. Not any longer."

"Why not?" Finally, the mysterious Esme explained. "Who is she? *What* is she?"

"Like you, Esme is half-Itari, but her father was human. Her mother died in the wars."

"Wars?"

"Wars. Centuries ago, more Itari lived on this plane with humans. We didn't interact that much, although some did. Intermarrying wasn't forbidden, but it was discouraged. In the 1300s, it came to a head. One of the Itari unleashed the Black Plague on the populace."

Eleanor gasped. The Black Plague had killed a third of the population before it finally petered out. "But...why?"

"They were tired of the barbaric nature of humans and felt that no matter how many centuries they waited, humans would never evolve to be worthy of this plane, its bounty, its beauty. The only answer was to wipe them out, but it backfired. Not only did it decimate the human population, it changed those who unleashed it. It altered the Itari's DNA until they became unrecognizable and are now what we call the Gehglers."

Her eyes widened. Gehglers were Itari? "Can they return to Itar?"

"No. They can travel the ley lines, but are trapped between parallel universes. They can spend time on this plane, but their energy doesn't allow them to cross to Itar. Some believe that the Gehglers can be returned to their former selves, but most of us don't. Esme's mother, a number of my friends, all became Gehglers."

If Esme's mother died in the 1300s, she was 800 years old. Esme was half human. Her stomach dropped. "Does that mean I—"

"It could. You could live over a thousand years."

A thousand years... Near immortality didn't appeal.

"Itari are one of the faerie kind from legends. We're not

really faeries, merely thought to be by humans. We live a long time. Much longer than humans."

"But I'm only *half* Itari."

He shrugged. "Most mixed blood live a little less than half that of an Itari. I am in my 30s-40s by our standards."

"And you? How old are you in human years?"

"Old enough to have seen the fall of the Roman Empire."

Her jaw nearly dropped, but, somehow, she managed to keep it shut and ask calmly, "But I thought you said your family has only been here for three generations?"

"It's true. I'm the third generation to have lived in this parallel universe and watched over its inhabitants. Our generations just happen to span more years than humans." He smiled.

She gave him a look that told him exactly what she thought of that and asked another question. "Have you spent your entire life here on this plane?"

He shook his head. "Most of it. My parents were on the side of those who wished to encourage the evolution of humans without interference. We see the potential in them. Yes, there is great evil, but there is also great good. In this digital age, it's much harder to stay in one place without being noticed. We 'aged', faked our deaths, and moved, or 'passed down' our land to other Itari and took over their land in past centuries. But, a few years ago, my parents decided to retire. They're in their twilight years and are tired of moving. They visit sometimes, but not that often anymore."

"And your brother? Why does he go to school?"

"Garth? He's a perpetual student, and it gives him something to do. He likes the young people. He says they keep his hope for humans alive."

She smiled. She didn't know Garth well, but it did seem like something he would say. "Is that why he stays here?"

"No. He's my backup. Should something happen to me, he is the second line of defense. He also keeps me strong, although it's not as necessary now that you're here."

She didn't say anything but just looked at him questioningly.

"My wife was one of those who believed that humans didn't deserve the earth. We argued about it a few times before the plague claimed her as well."

"Oh, Michael," she touched his arm, "I'm so sorry."

"Me, too," he said quietly. His intense, golden gaze bored into her. "I grieved for centuries, but, had she not, I would never have known you. There are reasons for everything. She is never coming back, and you are my future."

He paused and collected himself before continuing. "Esme believes your *fesuhn* can undo what the plague did to her mother. She has convinced the Gehglers that it will. It won't. There are those of us who have tried. Nothing can save them now. Since the plague, only a few Itari families remain here. We stay to ensure that no one else interferes, as we did, and to keep a watch on the Gehglers. The keepers help us do this."

"Why not rid the world of the Gehglers? And why am I being charged with this, if it was your kind that created them in the first place?" Anger rose within her. How dare they give her an ultimatum when this whole thing was their fault?

"They don't like to acknowledge the errors our kind has made, but getting rid of them is not that easy. And they have been in the background for the most part until your arrival. The *Ganginn*—"

"*Ganginn*?"

"Ruling body. They are also angry at your father for breaking the rules and siring you, for giving you such a powerful and rare *fesuhn*. It complicates things."

"According to Rodney, the Gehglers had chased everyone off that property. Why wait for so long to do something about me?"

"I don't know why they waited so long. The *Ganginn* don't tell me everything. The Gehglers have never gone after anyone like they have with you. Mostly, they just scare them enough to make them move. They've been waiting for someone like you. This area attracts those with power. It was only a matter of time."

"But what would my power do for them? They have Esme. And how could they know I would come and have this?" She pulled the *fesuhn* out from under her shirt. Light swirled and pulsed within the opalescent stone.

He stared at it hard, his eyes narrowing. "Something has

activated it."

Over his shoulder, the flower pulsed and shot out a sparkling ribbon of light that arced toward them. The ribbon undulated through the air and, starting at her feet, spiraled up her body like yarn on a spool until it completely encircled her. The smell of heavenly jasmine teased her senses. Ethereal singing swelled and reverberated in the chamber. Her ears buzzed, and every cell in her body vibrated and sung with it.

She closed her eyes in ecstasy, reaching her arms toward the ceiling with her head back. Power coursed through her. Sparkles of light danced behind her eyelids, and the answer came to her.

The energy slowly receded until only an echo remained. When she opened her eyes, Michael stared at her, mouth agape. The *fesuhn* glowed softly.

He reached for the pendant, but quickly drew his hand back when Eleanor felt a surge of energy from it.

"This is no ordinary *fesuhn*. I don't know where your father found this, but this one... *Falif Leia*," somber eyes looked into hers, "have the wars begun again?"

"No. Someone may want war, but it won't begin again." An underlying determination combined with the certainty that she could prevent any more wars, infused her with renewed energy. "It's unnecessary."

"You don't know what you're dealing with."

She looked down at her hands. What could she tell him? How did she explain to him what had been revealed to her? Now, she understood why forgiveness played a role. Without it, she wouldn't be able to take the next step. It was time to begin. She strode toward the door.

"Eleanor..."

Turning to face Michael, she said, "There's no time to talk about this. Are you coming?"

His eyes widened, and his mouth opened and shut before he nodded and moved to follow her.

She swallowed a chuckle and proceeded through the door, down the hallway, and all the way to the living room in the house above. Poor Michael. He wasn't used to this decisive Eleanor. She wasn't used to her either, but she liked her. This was the person she'd dreamed of being her entire life. Could it last? It had to. Everything else depended on it.

Chapter Thirty-Four

Not giving herself a chance to change her mind, Eleanor grabbed her coat from the closet by the front door and put it on.

"What are you doing?" Michael asked from behind her.

She glanced over her shoulder and said, "Going out."

"Eleanor..."

She faced him and smiled. "Trust me."

Before he could say anything else, she opened the door and stepped outside into the fog. Just beyond the edge of the trees, a mass of small, dark figures writhed like a nest of snakes, churning the mist into a roiling cauldron. A keening arose from the trees, and the Gehglers moved en masse into the clearing. Esme stood in the middle at the front. She smiled and held out her hand.

"Give me the *fesuhn*, Eleanor, and we'll leave you alone. We're growing tired of waiting."

For a moment, doubt assailed Eleanor. What was she doing? But, then, power surged through her, and euphoric singing rang in her ears. An intense feeling of love threaded through the power.

Her confidence soared, and the fear and doubt receded. "No, Esme. It's over."

Esme laughed. "You think you can fight *all* of us? You are a stupid human."

They advanced on her.

"There will be no fighting today." Eleanor raised her hands, palms outward. White light shot out from her palms, encircling Esme and the Gehglers. They froze.

Behind her, Michael gasped.

Eleanor ignored him and spoke, repeating the words swirling in her mind, *"Shelig dorus carim dar. Veri goru tellic gar. Grom di Ganginn, Sharhon, Dungis, i Lamati. Grom dan."*

The air shimmered in front of them. Twelve Itari materialized next to Esme. The Itari looked around them,

180

and cries of surprise filled the air. One of them turned to face her, anger quickly replacing his shocked expression.

"Why are we here?" He looked past her to Michael who stood behind her. "What is the meaning of this, Mykeli?"

"I—"

"I am responsible for this, Zonin. Michael has nothing to do with it," Eleanor said, drawing the tall, older Itari's attention away from Michael.

"You?" He studied her, his gaze stopping at the *fesuhn*. Thick, white eyebrows rose above cold, golden eyes. "Who gave you that?"

"My father, Tomani."

He scowled. "He has broken yet another rule. He will be—"

Anger swirled inside of her. The energy from the *somel* coursed through her, soothing her raging emotions. *Release the anger, Eleanor. You cannot win with anger.*

Eleanor gasped, but knew the voice was right. With a deep breath, she let it go and said, "—left alone."

His eyes narrowed. "Who are you to tell us how to discipline our race?"

"Who are the Itari to interfere with humans? You hold yourselves above us, then nearly destroy us and leave us with the wreckage of your experiment because you are unwilling to accept the responsibility for what you have done." She motioned to Sharhon. "Sharhon and her cohorts demanded I fix the mess your race made nearly a millennium ago or face the consequences. I have two more days, but I figured I'd get it done now. No time like the present."

Everyone turned to look at the tall, beautiful Itari at the end of the group.

Sharhon laughed mockingly and said, "We did no such thing. Are you going to believe a half-breed over me?"

"You forget that I was there, Sharhon." Michael stepped forward to stand next to Eleanor.

"*Sleeping* with her," Sharhon snarled.

A collective gasp arose from the Itari. Esme barked a laugh.

"*Loving* her, Sharhon. There is a difference, although you may not know it," Michael said and rested his hand on Eleanor's shoulder. His energy joined that of the *somel* pulsing through her, flushing the remaining anger out of her completely.

"You've seen yourselves as better than humans, more evolved. At one time, the Itari may have been. Certainly, your powers are, but that doesn't make you *better* than humans or our masters. Since the plague, your race has stagnated. Your denial of the damage caused by the plague you unleashed on this plane and your constant fighting over whether to allow humans to live or not—when it's not your decision to make— has changed you. The loving Itari you imagine yourself to be have grown arrogant and cold. Humans are not less than us. They are many things and capable of greatness, but not *less*. Itari are capable of greatness, too, but you have soiled your energy by refusing to face your flaws. To redeem your race, you must recognize what you've done and forgive yourselves."

The entire line of the *Ganginn* bristled. A cacophony of protests saturated the air. Esme snickered, and something lit in her eyes.

"*Us?* You are not Itari, Eleanor. Do not include yourself with *us*," Sharhon said, her voice dripping with scorn.

Staying calm and in a loving space grew harder each time Sharhon spoke, but Eleanor wouldn't let her get to her. She couldn't. Their lives depended on it. "I am half Itari, Sharhon. My father, Tomani, is Itari, but that isn't important." She turned her attention to the *Ganginn*. "Are you aware that Sharhon, Dungis, and Lamati wish to start the war again?"

"What?" Zonin and the other members of the *Ganginn* faced the three Itari who drew back from them.

"She lies, Zonin. What would we have to gain?" Even though Sharhon denied Eleanor's statement, her entire body tensed, and she looked away.

"Do not try to lie to the *Ganginn*," one member of the ruling body said. "We know the truth. You know what this means, Sharhon."

She shook her head and smiled. It dripped with condescension. "You can't, Daron. You don't have the power. None of you do." Sharhon motioned to Esme, but Esme didn't move. "Esme, what's wrong with you? Come here."

Esme stayed where she was.

Irritation in her every move, Sharhon turned her gaze to Eleanor. Her eyes widened, and she gasped. "So Esme was right. You have the *Giningeri fesuhn*. But you are nothing but a low creature not deserving even of this plane. None of your kind is. Why would you have it?" She spat in the dirt.

Eleanor struggled with the rage that blossomed within her. A loud popping sound filled the clearing as the energy receded, releasing Esme and the Gehglers. A mournful wailing arose from the Gehglers. It built into a howl and reverberated through the air. In the distance, a pack of coyotes answered with a chorus of their own.

Stay connected. Let the rage flow through and out of you until only peace remains. If she angers you, she wins.

Michael squeezed her shoulder and whispered in her ear, "Ignore her, *michu*. She is full of pain and envy. Like me, she lost her mate to the plague."

Compassion replaced the rage, and power poured back into her. It electrified every cell in her body and overflowed in a visible circle around her.

The energy prickled along her skin. When she opened her mouth to speak, white light flowed out with her words. "It has been decided that your kind can no longer live on this plane. You will have no access to this plane, except for those who currently live here and have proven their love for human kind. Every Itari will be returned home, including the Gehglers."

Everyone spoke at once in dissent. The Gehglers swayed and moved as if to attack her, but Esme motioned for them to stay back. Black eyes full of malice and hunger stared at her.

"Silence," Zonin yelled, his gaze ablaze with indignation. When the outcry receded, he continued. "Who are you to tell us what we can and cannot do? We have guarded you and your kind for centuries, human. How dare you assume to tell *us* what to do?"

As one, the *Ganginn* raised their hands, and beams of light poured out of them. The shafts joined and streamed straight for Eleanor. She raised her arms to shield herself and braced for the onslaught. A few moments passed, and nothing happened. Confused, she lowered her arms and gasped. The beams were hitting the bubble of energy around her and disbursing into it, dancing and sparkling harmlessly. The longer the *Ganginn* attacked, the brighter the air grew from charged energy. Her skin prickled from the power, and her hair stood on end. The *fesuhn* pulsed against her chest.

"*Gather the power, Eleanor,*" the voice whispered in her mind.

How did one gather power? Unsure of what to do, she lifted her arms over her head and spoke, "Come to me, *o somel tsho*. Fill me with your magnificence."

The energy coalesced into a gigantic, scintillating shape. It floated in front of them. Silver threads of light twisted within the amorphous mass like ribbons swirling in a maelstrom. The threads merged into a silver river that flowed toward Eleanor, encircling her and infusing her with so much power and love she felt as if it streamed from every pore in her body. The thoughts and emotions of every being in the clearing revealed themselves to her.

Fear, awe, anger assaulted her, but the *somel* continued to fill Eleanor with love so pure it burned through the other emotions. She opened her mouth, but no sound came out, only the light. The energy flowed out of her in a steady roar.

The *Ganginn* looked at each other, their eyes widening and dropped their hands to their sides. Their attack ceased, but the power grew within Eleanor and spread further and further around her, closing in on the Itari and Gehglers.

"Get her," Esme screamed and pointed at Eleanor.

The Gehglers rushed toward her, but, as they collided with the light, they were lifted in the air and hung suspended. Howls of rage and terror echoed through the clearing.

The air shimmered around the *Ganginn*, a portal opening, and Esme stepped back.

With a wave of her hand, Eleanor shut the portal. "You can't leave yet. We're not done here."

They glared at her, but the energy rolled over them, holding them in place.

"It is upon you to free the Gehglers from their chains. It is upon you to stop blaming humans for your errors. It is upon you to forgive and to love. Had you not meddled in human affairs, perhaps we would be more evolved. Perhaps not, but we'll never know because you did. It no longer matters. We are where we are. If we destroy ourselves within a few centuries, you'll still be alive. However, you won't be able to return until you've solved your own issues, healed your own wounds, and saved the Gehglers. Only those pure of heart and mind will be able to crossover. The rest of you won't."

"Who are you to judge us?" Sharhon ground out. "You know nothing of loss."

Eleanor raised her chin and said, "Who are you to judge *us*, Sharhon? Look what your judgment has gained you." She motioned to the Gehglers. "Your loss was created by your arrogance, but the next choices you make can change everything."

She paused and looked around the clearing before speaking again. "A very wise man told me that I would not be able to resolve my issues until I forgave myself. He was right." She smiled at the thought of her father. Compassion mixed with the love again. Forgiveness was hard. The only reason she had forgiven herself was because she had no choice. Well, the choice was between life and death. She'd chosen life. Hopefully, they would, too.

The other woman scowled, but said nothing.

"Forgiveness will set you free, Sharhon. It will set all of you free." She let her gaze connect with each Itari and Gehgler before her. "Now, you must go home."

"But—" Zonin began, his face bright red.

Eleanor ignored him and raised her arms. The air shimmered. Through the portal, the verdant forests of Itar appeared.

"*Varter gan zo Itar*. You're not welcome here anymore. There's no room for you here. Be gone."

She flicked her wrists, and the *Ganginn*, the Gehglers, Esme, and Sharhon and her partners were pushed through the opening. Cries of outrage accompanied their departure. The portal closed, and they disappeared.

Arms still outstretched, Eleanor said in Itari, "The portal shall stay closed to all Itari and any other beings who come with intent to harm this plane or its inhabitants or to interfere with human evolution."

Dropping her arms to her sides, she turned to Michael. Awe comingled with love in his eyes. She smiled at him. The energy receded, and exhaustion poured in. Swaying, she took a step and stumbled. He caught her as she toppled forward.

Epilogue

A few months later

"Do you, Michael Donald Stevens, take this woman to be your lawfully wedded wife? To have and to hold from this day forward for as long as you both shall live?" her best friend Jennifer asked.

"I do."

His deep voice sent shivers down her spine.

"Do you, Eleanor Helen Radcliffe, take this man to be your lawfully wedded husband? To have and to hold from this day forward for as long as you both shall live?"

"I do."

"Then I now pronounce you husband and wife. You may kiss the bride," Jennifer said with a grin.

Michael lowered his head and claimed her lips. Eyes closed, she gave herself over to the sensations his touch always created. A cheer rose from the small gathering in the backyard of their ranch house that included her father, and the couple drew apart.

Eleanor gazed into her husband's face. Love infused every part of her being. The past two months had been amazing. Forgiving herself and others had been the best decision she'd ever made. Not that there weren't challenges, or wouldn't be more, but they would get through them together. And she could live with that.

www.ingramcontent.com/pod-product-compliance
Lightning Source LLC
Chambersburg PA
CBHW061208170626
46809CB00003B/1286